KAYLA O'BRIAN
TROUBLE AT BITTER CREEK RANCH

Other Crossway Books by
Hilda Stahl

THE PRAIRIE FAMILY ADVENTURE SERIES

Sadie Rose and the Daring Escape
Sadie Rose and the Cottonwood Creek Orphan
Sadie Rose and the Outlaw Rustlers
Sadie Rose and the Double Secret
Sadie Rose and the Mad Fortune Hunters
Sadie Rose and the Phantom Warrior
(more to follow)

THE SUPER J*A*M SERIES

The Great Adventures of Super J*A*M
The World's Greatest Hero

GROWING UP ADVENTURES

Sendi Lee Mason and the Milk Carton Kids
Sendi Lee Mason and the Stray Striped Cat
Sendi Lee Mason and the Big Mistake
(more to follow)

KAYLA O'BRIAN ADVENTURES

Kayla O'Brian and the Dangerous Journey

(more to follow)

A KAYLA O'BRIAN ADVENTURE

Kayla O'Brian
TROUBLE AT BITTER CREEK RANCH

Hilda Stahl

CROSSWAY BOOKS • WHEATON, ILLINOIS
A DIVISION OF GOOD NEWS PUBLISHERS

Kayla O'Brian: Trouble at Bitter Creek Ranch.

Published by Crossway Books, a division of
Good News Publishers, Wheaton, Illinois 60187.

Series design: Ad Plus; Cover illustration: David Acquistapace

First printing, 1991

Printed in the United States of America

ISBN 0-89107-611-5

99 98 97 96 95 94 93 92 91
15 14 13 12 11 10 9 8 7 6 5 4 3 2 1

Dedicated with love
to three special women of God—
my daughters,

Kathy
Dawn
Jan

Contents

The Orphan Train 1

Ignoring the noise of the orphans, Kayla held Mama's diary and Bible in her lap and stroked them just as Mama had stroked her hair when she'd had trouble falling asleep on the voyage from Ireland. The two books were all she and Timothy had left of Mama and Papa. Tears filled Kayla's eyes, but she quickly blinked them away before the others saw and scoffed.

Suddenly Ear, a six-year-old with half his left ear gone, snatched the diary from Kayla, and Louie, a seven-year-old with a withered hand, grabbed the Bible.

"No! Stop!" cried Kayla in great anguish as she lunged at Ear and Louie. "Give me back Mama's Bible and diary!" Her shout was lost in the clack and rumble of the train and the laughing and shouting of the other orphans that filled the boxcar. The Children's Aid Society had collected the orphans in the streets of New York City and were taking them west to find families and a new life.

"You'll never see your mama's Bible or diary again!" yelled Louie as he and Ear easily slipped among the crowd. They'd lived on the streets the last three years and were alive today because they'd learned to use a knife, pick pockets, and disappear into thin air.

Frantically Kayla pushed through the ragged, dirty orphans in the boxcar that seemed to stretch on for miles. She had to get Mama's Bible and diary back!

Standing on tiptoe, Kayla stretched her neck and looked around for her brother Timothy. She finally saw him fighting with two big boys. She shouted his name, but he didn't hear, and no one else paid any attention to her either.

Suddenly someone opened the sliding door of the boxcar. Bright sunlight and cool, fresh air rushed in.

"Kayla O'Brian!" shouted Ear and Louie, standing in the open doorway with the diary and Bible held high. "Look!"

Kayla screamed as they flung the diary and Bible out of the boxcar and into the field at the side of the track. The pages fluttered in the wind. "No! No!" she cried.

"And your brother goes too!" The two big boys pitched Timothy out the door as if he were a rag doll.

"Timothy!" Kayla leaped forward to catch him — and sailed right out the open door, her long skirts whipping around her legs.

Suddenly she felt someone grab her arm and shake her hard. She sat up quickly and found she wasn't falling off the Orphan Train at all. She was sitting in the backseat of a swaying buggy, with Timothy safe beside her. Instead of the clack of the train, she heard the rattle of harness and the creak of the buggy. Instead of the stuffy boxcar, she saw stretching on and on before her a waving sea of grass and darkening sky that reached down, down to touch the green waves.

"Kayla, wake up!" whispered Timothy, shaking her harder.

She gripped his hand tightly. A chilly wind tangled her mass of black hair, and she clasped the ugly brown coat from the Children's Aid Society even closer around her. "I'm awake now, Timothy. 'Tis a nightmare I was having! But it seemed as real as the green hills of Ireland!"

"Are you all right?" he asked in a hushed voice as he cast a glance toward the front seat of the buggy where Rachel Larsen sat with the reins in her hands.

"That I am," whispered Kayla. It wouldn't do for him to know how frightened she often felt ever since that terrible day when they'd buried Mama and Papa at sea. Being the older, she had to look after him. "I dreamed we were back on the train and Ear and Louie took Mama's diary and Bible."

Timothy grinned. "'Tis something Ear and Louie would do. They'll be a handful to the family who took them."

Kayla peeked through her long, dark lashes at Rachel Larsen, who had stopped at the Orphan Train and signed for them both even though she'd expected to get a big strong boy. Rachel wore a long gray coat, a faded calico bonnet, and cowboy boots on her feet. She was quite tall and slender and had a plain face. Kayla turned back to Timothy. "Have we been riding long?"

Timothy huddled deeper into his coat. "I don't know. I was asleep for a while."

"Did she talk to you at all?" whispered Kayla, nodding toward Rachel Larsen.

"Not one word has she spoken." Timothy leaned his head against Kayla's so his words wouldn't carry to the front seat of the open buggy. "Maybe she's sorry she took us."

"And why would she be?"

"Because I'm still short and skinny!" That was a sore spot with Timothy.

"You will grow to be a big strapping man like Papa." Kayla squeezed Timothy's hand. "And if you don't grow that much, it will not matter. That the inner man be strong in the Lord is of greater value."

"I know," said Timothy. But he still wanted his outer man to be big and strong like Papa had been. Just then Timothy glanced at the team. He'd been trying not to look at it. That was another sore spot. "Kayla, did you see the team?"

Kayla nodded. She hadn't wanted to say anything about them.

"Mules," said Timothy in great disappointment. "Why would a rancher drive mules?"

"That I don't know."

"Granddad always said, 'There are three things that can't be ruled — a mule, a pig, and a woman.'" Timothy sighed heavily. "Mules! I want to be a cowboy on a horse like we've seen from the boxcar. What cowboy would ride a mule?"

Kayla giggled at the picture she saw in her mind. "Mules aren't all that bad. You liked Grandma's mule."

"I know." Timothy frowned at the brown mules plodding along at a steady pace. "But horses I know and understand . . . Mules I don't."

"I wonder what the kids will be like," whispered Kayla. Rachel had said at the train that she had two boys, fifteen and five, and two girls, eleven and six.

"That I've been wondering myself." Timothy was quiet a long time. "Mules, Kayla!"

"God has given us strength to handle even mules," said Kayla.

"That I have my doubts about," muttered Timothy, dragging his eyes off the mules.

Several minutes later, after darkness had already fallen, Rachel Larsen drove into the ranch yard and stopped outside the big barn. Light shone from a window of the house. A screen door squawked and a man called, "That you, Rachel?"

"It's me, Abel," she called back.

"You got that orphan kid with you?"

Timothy stiffened, and Kayla gripped his hand.

Rachel hesitated. "That's what you sent me for."

"Have him stay in the barn and watch over Sterling. Somebody's been sneakin' around again." The door slammed, and all was quiet.

Rachel climbed from the buggy. "You two sleep in the barn tonight."

As she stepped from the buggy Kayla wanted to ask about Sterling, but she could hear by Rachel's voice that she was worn out.

Inside the barn Rachel lit a lantern and hung it on a peg on the nearest stall. "Bring your stuff in here."

Timothy and Kayla carried their bags inside, helped unhitch the mules, and watched as Rachel put them in the pen beside the barn.

"Sleep in here," said Rachel, waving at a nearby stall. "Sterling's over there." She pointed to the stall beside them, where a white mule stood. "Somebody's after him." Every word she spoke seemed to be forced out of her. It was as if words had hardened inside her and couldn't break free.

She pulled two blankets off a rack and dropped them on the dirt floor of the stall. "The toilet's on the path between here and the house on the other side of the shed. The well is to the right of the barn." She lifted a full gunnysack out of the buggy. "I'll be back out after daylight."

Kayla watched Rachel walk away into the darkness toward the house. She heard the screen door squawk, then silence.

Timothy stared at the big white mule as if his dreams had been shattered. "Why would anybody want to steal a mule?"

"He's a fine-looking fellow," said Kayla with a laugh. "He can't help it if he's a mule." She looked around thoughtfully. "I'm thinking we should sleep right here at Sterling's stall door to alert us to any nighttime visitors." She spread some loose hay over the floor, shook out the blankets, and spread them out. "Tonight we sleep without the noise and sway of the train or the snoring of the others."

"But we sleep with the chance of a mule thief coming," said Timothy. He rummaged around in his case and pulled out the cudgel that had more than once saved his life on the streets of New York City. He'd never told Kayla about his fights or how near death he'd come. She would've worried too much about him, and she already felt responsible enough for him.

Several minutes later Kayla curled up in her blanket with Timothy in his beside her. Sterling moved around in the stall. An owl hooted. Without the soft glow of the lantern the barn was in total darkness. Kayla lay still, then once again felt the sway of the train. She closed her eyes, and the noise of the orphans rang in her head. Silently she thanked God for the home he'd provided for Timothy and herself and that they were still together.

Timothy held the cudgel close to him and stared into

the darkness. It was too quiet. Even with Kayla nearby he suddenly felt lonely and even frightened. In all his thirteen years he'd slept with others nearby. Back in County Offaly Mama, Papa, Granddad, and Grandma had slept in the same house. In the ship coming across the Atlantic there were rows of bunk beds, all full of people. At the Murphys' in New York City the tiny room had been wall to wall with Murphys — and in the boxcar coming west wall to wall orphans. Timothy moved restlessly. What would Kayla think of him if she knew how he felt? Could he fall asleep in such a quiet, lonely place?

Kayla listened to the wind blowing through the rafters of the barn. Would she hear someone coming in? At a strange sound she lifted her head. Was that the creak of the door? Had someone slipped inside? She held her breath and listened. Her heart hammered so loud she was sure Timothy could hear it. Finally she settled back down, her head close to her bag that held Mama's diary and Bible. 'Twould be perfect if Mama and Papa were here and not in Heaven. If they'd survived the trip, they'd all be together in Maryland at Briarwood Farms, working with horses. Papa had been one of the best trainers in all of Ireland.

Tears welled up in Kayla's eyes. Oh, how she missed Papa and Mama! A tear slipped down the side of her face and dampened her hair. She frowned and quickly brushed away the wetness. She would not feel sorry for herself and give in to tears! Her strength and peace and comfort came from God, her Heavenly Father. Papa had told her many times, "When you let Jesus into your life, you became a child of the King! You are more than a conqueror through Jesus Christ our Lord. You can do all things through Christ who gives you strength. Never, never let Satan defeat you. No attack from

Satan can defeat you unless you allow it to. You are God's child, a child of the King!"

Kayla's heart leaped, and she smiled into the darkness. She and Timothy belonged to the King of the universe! They were not alone! They could conquer anything, even mules!

The Larsen Family 2

Kayla sat up with a start and shivered with cold. Light was filtering through the cracks in the barn. It was morning already! She checked to make sure Sterling was still in the stall. She saw his breath hanging in the air. She smiled, then reached out to wake Timothy. He was rolled in a ball to keep warm.

He sat up slowly and rubbed his eyes.

"Top of the morning to you, Timothy O'Brian," she said with a twinkle in her blue eyes. Straw clung to her mass of black hair. "'Tis time to get presentable and go meet our new family."

Timothy leaned against the stall door and looked at Sterling. "I was hoping it was a bad dream," he said. "I was hoping you were a bad dream, Sterling . . . Or that somebody stole you away while we slept."

Kayla laughed and rumpled Timothy's already tangled hair. "Don't you be giving Sterling anything to fear."

Sterling shook his head, and his rope halter flopped slightly.

"You be taking care of your blanket before Rachel Larsen gets here, Timothy."

"Why?" asked Timothy as he picked up the blanket.

"We want her to know O'Brians are not ones to stay abed in the morning. Nor are O'Brians lazy." Kayla picked up her blanket, shook it out, folded it properly, and put it back in place.

"Sometimes it's hard to be an O'Brian," muttered Timothy as he made sure the blanket was folded neatly enough to satisfy Kayla.

Just then the barn door opened, and Rachel Larsen stepped in. A man's old brown hat covered her dark blonde hair, and her long coat flapped around her long legs.

"Good morning, Rachel Larsen!" Kayla and Timothy said at the same time, then laughed. "Good morning," said Kayla again.

A flicker of surprise passed over Rachel's plain face, but she didn't smile. She walked to Sterling, patted his neck, and nodded, then turned to Kayla and Timothy. "Bring your stuff and come inside for breakfast."

"I'm hungry enough to eat . . ." Timothy glanced at Sterling, grinned, then shook his head. He wasn't quite that hungry! "Hungry enough to eat a whole stack of flapjacks," he finished.

Kayla grabbed up her bag and fell into step beside Rachel. The sun was peeking over the hills. The ground was covered with frost. A rooster crowed from the fence outside the chicken house. Kayla breathed deeply, thankful for fresh, crisp air, so much better than the stale air of the boxcar full of orphans. She smiled at Rachel as they followed the path toward the house. "You look rested and well this fine morning."

Rachel kept on walking.

"What would you be having us call you?" asked Kayla.

Rachel didn't lose a step. "Rachel. That's my name."

"And a fine name it 'tis," said Timothy from just behind them. He craned his neck to look all around in hopes of spotting a horse. He saw several mules grazing in a pasture, chickens scratching in the grass, and a donkey in a pen by himself. "Where are the horses?" he asked just as they reached the back door of the house.

"In a corral in back of the barn," said Rachel.

Timothy grinned and squared his shoulders. Now that was more like it!

The door opened right into the warm, roomy kitchen. Smells of coffee, frying bacon, eggs, and biscuits made Timothy's stomach growl with hunger and Kayla's mouth water.

Kayla stopped a few steps inside the door. Four kids and a man who needed a shave sat at the table, and they were all staring at her as if she had two heads. She slipped off her coat, and still they stared. "And am I that funny to look at?" she asked with a laugh. "I know my hair needs a good brushing and I slept in my clothes, but I didn't know I was a sight enough to leave you speechless."

"Who is this?" asked the man.

Timothy frowned slightly. No one had given him more than a glance. He couldn't see a thing wrong with Kayla to cause such a stir.

Rachel lifted her head a fraction, pulled off her battered hat and her long coat, and dropped them on a chair. Her cheeks were rosy from the cold. "She's Kayla O'Brian," said Rachel. She motioned to Timothy. "Timothy O'Brian. They're brother and sister." Rachel waved toward the kids and the man. "Abel Larsen and the kids oldest to youngest — Greene, Jane, Ula, and Scott."

Kayla smiled at the Larsens, but no one smiled back.

"I sent you after a boy," said Abel, scowling.

"They came as a pair," said Rachel, filling her cup with coffee. She nodded toward two empty chairs. "Sit and eat."

Kayla and Timothy sat at the table, suddenly feeling out of place. Weren't they wanted after all?

"I sent you after a full-growed boy!" roared Abel, pounding the table with his fist.

Rachel only shrugged.

"Timothy's a hard worker, even if he is small," said Kayla brightly.

Abel glowered at her. "I wasn't talkin' to you."

"I might be small now, but I'll grow," said Timothy.

"Not if you don't keep your yap shut 'til you're spoke to!"

Abel turned back to Rachel as she sat at the last empty chair. "What made you bring back these two?"

Rachel forked three fried eggs onto her plate.

"We were all that was left," said Kayla in a steady voice. "Don't go blaming her. She did the best she could."

The sudden silence at the table sent a chill down Kayla's spine, but she looked Abel Larsen square in the eye. Finally he leaned back and rubbed his whiskery chin.

"What'd you say your name was?" asked Abel.

"Kayla O'Brian." Kayla smiled at Timothy. "And my brother Timothy. I'm fourteen and he's thirteen. He'll have a growth spurt one of these days and be the strapping big lad that you want. I had mine on the voyage. Outgrew all my clothes and had to wear Mama's." Kayla's voice broke a little at the mention of Mama, and the familiar longing stabbed her heart.

"Eat," said Rachel, handing a plate of eggs to Kayla.

Kayla and Timothy filled their plates and ate.

"Did you have any trouble last night?" asked Abel when he finished eating.

"Over Sterling, you mean?" asked Timothy.

Abel nodded.

"Not a bit." Timothy leaned back. "Why would anyone steal a mule?"

Abel laughed, but it wasn't a pleasant laugh. "Words from my own mouth!"

Rachel scraped back her chair and stood. "Sterling is worth several hundred dollars!" The tone of her voice made it obvious that she was saying, "Drop the subject." She settled her hat in place. "Jane, show them where they'll be sleeping tonight."

"Where, Ma?" asked Jane in a low, shy voice.

Rachel frowned. "Kayla with you girls, Timothy with the boys."

"One of 'em will have to keep watch over Sterling," said Abel. "Or maybe the two together since you didn't bring home a big boy like I asked for."

"I'll sleep out there tonight," said Rachel coldly.

"Sleep where you will," snapped Abel. "Greene, help me up!"

Greene blushed and kept his head down as he walked over to Abel.

Greene was as tall and muscled as Abel with black hair that needed cutting and sad blue eyes. He wrapped his arm around Abel and lifted.

With a cane in one hand and Greene on the other,

Abel made it to the rocking chair in the front room. He sat down heavily, and Greene slid a footstool under his outstretched leg.

Kayla and Timothy followed Jane up the closed-in, narrow stairs. Jane was thin with blonde hair and blue eyes that didn't sparkle. "The boys' room," she said and pushed open a heavy paneled door. The room was large and messy with two beds, a wardrobe, and two dressers.

Timothy set his case inside and walked with them to the girls' room. It was also large and messy, with two beds, a wardrobe, two dressers, and a free-standing looking glass with a dress draped over it.

"Which bed will I sleep on?" asked Kayla. She couldn't wait to clean the room.

"This is mine, and that one's Ula's. Take your pick."

"I could sleep on the floor."

Jane shrugged. "It don't matter none."

Kayla set her case against a wall near a big dresser. "Will I have a drawer to myself?"

Jane opened two empty drawers. "You can have these. We don't have nothing to put in them."

Kayla wanted a safe place for Mama's diary and Bible. Would the others look at her things when she wasn't around? Finally she emptied her case and bag into the drawers, making sure the diary and Bible were in the very back of a drawer with one of Mama's dresses over it.

"How old are you, Jane?" asked Timothy. She was the same height as he was and just as thin.

She blushed. "Eleven."

Timothy shrugged. "How about Greene?"

"Fifteen."

"I hope I'm that big when I'm fifteen," said Timothy.

"Ula is six, and Scott is five," said Jane before Timothy could ask.

"What happened to your papa's leg?" asked Kayla.

"Mule kicked him a couple of weeks back."

Just then Rachel yelled up the stairs, "What's keeping you kids?"

"We got to hurry," said Jane. Her blonde braids bouncing on her thin back, she led the way downstairs to the front room where the others were waiting.

Rachel motioned to Timothy. "Greene and Scott will show you around and tell you your chores."

Timothy slapped Greene on the back. "Let's go . . . I want a look at your horses."

Greene looked at Timothy strangely, but didn't say anything.

"I'll show 'em to you," said Scott. He was short and plump with white hair and wide blue eyes. He ran for the door, and Timothy and Greene followed.

Rachel brushed a strand of blonde hair off her sunbrowned cheek. Her face was long and narrow just like she was. "Jane, you work with me. Kayla, you help Ula clean the house and make dinner. If you have any questions Ula can't answer, ask Abel."

Abel lowered his newspaper. "Don't bother me if I'm asleep. Didn't get much last night."

"Is there anything I can get you? More coffee? A glass of water?" asked Kayla.

"Well now," said Abel in surprise.

"Don't wait on him," said Rachel sharply. "He could walk if he wanted."

Abel slapped the paper hard against the arm of the big

oak rocking chair. "You know better 'n that, woman! My legs are crippled up from that blasted mule!"

Rachel walked out without another word, and Jane ran after her.

Ula tugged Kayla into the kitchen and whispered, "Are you a real orphan?"

Kayla's stomach knotted. How she hated to be called an orphan! "My mama and papa are in Heaven."

"But are you a real orphan?"

Kayla barely nodded.

Ula motioned for Kayla to bend down to her, then whispered in Kayla's ear, "Sometimes I wish I was."

Kayla looked shocked. "It's sad to be an orphan, Ula."

"It's sad to be me too," Ula said with giant tears in her eyes.

"But you live on a nice ranch in a nice house. You have a mama and papa."

Ula bit her bottom lip, then whispered, "I want a mama to hug me and kiss me and a papa to swing me high in his arms. One time in town I saw a girl my size with a ma and pa like that."

Kayla gathered Ula in her arms and held her tight. "I can't be your mama, but I can give you hugs and kisses."

Ula pulled away, her face red. "You won't tell on me, will you? Them others would make fun of me."

"I won't tell. Now let's get to work. We want this place to shine!"

Ula stared at Kayla in surprise. "Don't you hate working?"

"Sometimes."

"I sure do!"

"I'll be having fun cleaning this grand house!" Kayla

walked to the stove to put water on to heat. "It's been a long time since I've lived in a real house with a real family."

Ula stacked the dirty plates. "Ma said you have to go help Grandma after dinner today." Ula shivered. "You won't like that at all!"

Kayla trembled. Just what was so terrible about their grandma?

Dinnertime

As Ula stepped outside to ring the dinner bell, Kayla stood before Abel in his rocking chair. "You are the man of the house, so 'tis only proper that I ask . . ."

Abel frowned up at her. His eyes were heavy from the nap he'd just taken. "Man of the house? That's a good one. Ask away."

Kayla locked her fingers behind her back and calmed the butterflies fluttering in her stomach. "Would it be too much to ask that we thank the Lord for our food before we eat?"

Abel's blue eyes widened. Then he laughed and nodded. "Rachel won't like it much, but we'll do it."

"Thank you!" Smiling, Kayla hurried back to the kitchen to dish up the food. They'd made fried chicken, potatoes, gravy, squash, green beans, and a big pan of biscuits. For dessert they'd baked four apple pies. The delicious smells swirled around the warm kitchen.

Kayla glanced out the window, looking for Timothy. The sky was overcast, and the wind blew tumbleweeds across the yard. The morning had hurried by with all the work she'd done, but she'd missed Timothy and wanted to make sure he was all right. Often he was too daring and did things to prove he wasn't too small for any task.

Finally Timothy walked in, flushed and excited. Greene kept his eyes down, but Scott ran in with a shout.

"Me and Timothy are hungry as two bears in winter," said Scott, dipping his hands in the washpan and rubbing them on the towel beside it. His white hair stood on end, and his round cheeks were red from the chilly wind.

"Get in here and help me to the table, Greene," shouted Abel.

Greene quickly washed and dried his hands and hurried to the front room.

"Something smells good, Kayla," said Timothy, sniffing as he walked around the table to look at the food.

"Did you see the horses?" asked Kayla as she set the sliced sweet pickles on the table next to the dill pickles.

Timothy grinned and nodded. "All mares. A couple of 'em are worth talking about." He rolled his eyes. "They have 'em as breeding stock only. This is a mule ranch! They train and sell mules!"

Kayla laughed as she tapped Timothy's shoulder. "'Tis not Briarwood Farms, but we're together with a fine roof over our heads."

"That we are," said Timothy just as Rachel and Jane walked in, looking tired and chilly.

Rachel stopped just inside the door and looked around in surprise at the clean kitchen and the bountiful meal.

With a proud look on her thin face Ula stepped closer to Kayla, waiting for praise from Rachel. But without a word Rachel washed and sat in her chair.

"They made apple pies, Ma," said Scott as he sat down.

"That's what I've been smelling," said Abel as he lowered himself to his chair with Greene's help.

Kayla smiled as she sat down, her hands folded in her lap while she looked expectantly at Abel.

He grinned like a mischievous boy, and when everyone was seated he said, "Kayla here asked if she could pray before we eat."

Rachel snorted and reached for the potatoes.

The others sat very still. Timothy bowed his head and folded his hands in his lap.

Kayla bowed her head and said, "Heavenly Father, thank You for this fine family and for the good food. It's blessed to our bodies in Jesus' name. Thank You for health and peace and joy. Amen." She lifted her head to find Jane and Greene staring at her. Rachel was quietly eating.

"Amen!" said Abel. He sounded ready to burst out laughing as he looked at Rachel. She didn't even flick an eyelash. With a scowl he reached for the chicken.

Timothy filled his plate, then bit into a crispy chicken leg. "Aw, Kayla O'Brian, you've outdone yourself this time."

"With Ula's help," said Kayla, smiling at Ula.

Ula smiled back, then ducked her head and took a big bite of potatoes and gravy.

As Kayla ate, the only sounds were chewing and the clinking of forks against plates. The silence stretched on and on. She glanced at Timothy, and by the twinkle in his eye she knew he knew she couldn't stand it a minute longer. "Ula and I had a fine time cleaning this morning," she said.

All eyes turned on her in surprise.

She chuckled and continued telling about the morning,

eating only while Timothy told about his morning outdoors and the mule their grandma in Ireland once had.

"Greene, what'd you say your donkey's name is?" asked Timothy after another long silence.

Greene glanced up, his face beet-red, then looked down at his apple pie. "Washington," he said in a low voice.

"George Washington," said Scott. "But we mostly call him Wash or Washington."

"That's a fine name," said Kayla.

"Ma named him," said Ula.

"She's good with names," said Jane. She blushed and sank down in her chair.

"What chatterboxes!" said Rachel, pushing away from the table. "Get a move on, Jane." Rachel reached for her hat on a peg by the back door, then turned to Kayla. "You go take care of Ma's chores this afternoon. Her name's Pansy Butler. Ula will show you where she lives."

Ula gasped.

Rachel frowned at her. "You don't have to go with Kayla. Just show her."

Ula sighed in relief.

Kayla's stomach tightened. Just what was wrong with Pansy Butler?

Abel chuckled drily. "You might lose some of that chipper talk and happy laugh after spending an afternoon with old Pansy."

Rachel glared at Abel, then slammed out of the house with Jane right behind her.

"Greene, take me outside for a while," said Abel gruffly.

After Abel and Greene walked out, Kayla slowly pushed back her chair. Something was terribly wrong between Abel and Rachel. They didn't act like they were deeply in love like Mama and Papa had been. Right then and there Kayla vowed she'd do all she could to help the two learn to care for one another.

Timothy jumped up and started helping clear the table. Ula and Scott stared at him in shock. He saw their looks and and lifted a dark brow "And do I have pie on my face or gravy spilled on my shirt?"

"Why are you doing woman's work?" asked Scott.

"He's a helper," said Kayla.

"I ate the food and dirtied the dishes, so I can help clean them up," said Timothy with a chuckle. "You can do the same, Scott. It's better than standing around with your hands in your pockets." Papa had always said that, and Timothy choked back a tiny sob that suddenly rose inside him.

Scott slowly reached for his plate to stack it on the others. He jabbed Ula's arm. "I'm not no girl just because I'm helping!"

"I didn't say you were! I help you herd the mules, don't I, and that don't make me no boy," said Ula with a flip of her braids.

Just then Greene poked his head in the door. Cool air rushed in around him. He wouldn't look at Kayla. "Timothy, Scott, come on. We got work to do."

Timothy set the handful of forks down beside the piled plates and hurried outdoors with Scott.

When they were all alone Ula said, "How come you talked at the table, Kayla?"

"It's good manners to," said Kayla. "Conversation and food . . . that's what a meal is about."

"Oh . . . Ma won't never let us talk."

Kayla stopped dead still. So that's why they all looked

at her so strangely. She burst out laughing. "I never had good manners get me in trouble before."

Ula rubbed soap into the pan of dishwater. "I think Ma likes you."

Kayla's heart jerked. "What makes you think so?"

"She didn't yell at you for talking."

"I think your ma works too hard. I think that's why she's so quiet."

"She's not a bit happy," said Ula.

"Oh?"

"I heard her tell Grandma so."

"That's too bad. We'll pray for her."

"Ma don't think much of praying either."

"God loves her anyway," said Kayla as she set the glasses in the dishpan.

Suddenly a shot rang out. Kayla almost dropped the glass in her hand. She ran to the door with Ula on her heels. Abel sat on a bench on the far end of the porch that ran across the whole front of the house and wrapped around the side.

"That was Rachel's gun," said Abel, frowning as he tried to stand. "Kayla, go see what's wrong. This dadblasted leg! . . . Can't be of help when I should be!"

"Ma's in the training corral," said Ula, pointing west of the barn.

Her heart hammering, Kayla ran to the corral and climbed on the top rail. Rachel stood with her rifle at her shoulder, aiming at the tall grass on the far side of the corral. Jane stood beside her, her hand over her mouth, her face as gray as the overcast sky. "What's wrong?" shouted Kayla just as Ula scrambled up beside her.

"A wild dog," said Rachel, lowering her rifle. "See for yourself. It fell there beside the post with the skull on it."

Kayla spotted the post with the skull of an ox or cow on top. "You stay back, Ula." Kayla jumped down and ran around the outside edge of the wooden fence until she saw the dog.

"Did you find it?" called Rachel.

"Yes." Kayla leaned down and looked the dog over. She couldn't see any blood. She nudged the dog with her toe. She saw its rib cage move and realized it was alive She looked closer. "Why, you're but a pup," she said softly. Its light brown hair was long, and it had a white circle around its right eye. Its paws were huge, showing it wasn't fully grown yet.

"Is it dead?" called Rachel.

"No," said Kayla, shaking her head.

"Take a stick and bash its head in!"

Kayla gasped. "That I will not do!" she cried. "'Tis a pup you shot." She looked closer and saw where the bullet had grazed the skull.

"A pup?" cried Jane. She ran toward Kayla and climbed the fence and jumped over. "Oh, it is a pup!"

Rachel climbed the fence and looked down at the dog. She raised the rifle to her shoulder and took aim.

"Don't!" cried Kayla, her eyes pleading with Rachel. "We'll make a fine watchdog out of him." She looked at Jane as she stroked the dog's large head and pointed ears. "And a fine pet too."

"Stand back!" snapped Rachel.

"Please, Ma," whispered Jane, giant tears in her eyes.

"'Tis but a pup, Rachel," said Kayla softly.

"It was after the young mules," said Rachel gruffly.

"We'll train him to guard the mules," said Kayla. "That I promise you."

Rachel looked down the barrel of the rifle, the sights leveled at the dog's brain. Suddenly she lowered the gun, turned on her heels, and walked away. On the other side of the fence she said over her shoulder, "Get that dog to the shed and take care of it. Be quick about it!"

Jane laughed shakily and flicked away her tears.

Kayla awkwardly lifted the dog and walked with Jane to the shed.

Pansy Butler

Kayla watched six-year-old Ula race back across the wide open prairie toward home. Then she turned toward the ranch house where Grandma Pansy Butler lived. Two barns, a windmill, a sod house, and three other small buildings stood a good distance from the house. The place looked deserted. Kayla took a deep breath, held her chin high, and walked out from behind the grassy knoll and into the open where anyone watching from the porch of the house or from a window could see her. The sun had come out and had chased away the gray sky. "Pansy Butler, I don't know what to expect of you, but here I come!" said Kayla. Then she laughed.

Kayla was almost to the three trees that stood north of the house when the door opened a crack and a rifle barrel poked out. Kayla stood still as fear pricked her skin. The barrel didn't waver even a fraction of an inch.

"You take one more step and I'll put a hole right between your eyes!" shouted Pansy Butler in a raspy voice. "Who are you, and what are you doing trespassing on my place?"

Her stomach flipping wildly, Kayla squared her shoulders and lifted her chin high. Wind tugged at her mass of black hair and the small ruffle around her bonnet. "I am Kayla O'Brian! I live with your daughter Rachel. She sent me here to do your chores."

"I don't believe you!"

Kayla's blue eyes flashed. "An O'Brian does not lie!"

"How'd you get here?"

"Ula showed me the way."

"Then she probably ran like the scared rabbit she is," snapped Pansy Butler. She opened the door further. "I'm sending my dog out. If Czar rips you to pieces I'll know I can't trust you."

Kayla bit back a gasp. Frantically she searched for something to say. "I've read of the czars of Russia."

Pansy Butler jerked open the door and stepped to the wide porch, the rifle against her plump shoulder, a big gold collie at her side. Pansy was short, with thin gray hair in wild tangles down to her shoulders. She wore a gray, patched wool dress, cowboy boots, and a wide belt around her middle with a revolver stuck in a leather holster. "What d' you know about Russia?"

"Only what I've read," said Kayla, forcing her voice to stay steady.

"Don't lie to me, girl! You can't read or write if you came from Rachel's house."

Kayla locked her knees to keep them from knocking. "I came from Ireland, and I can read and I can write."

Pansy lowered her rifle, touched the collie's head, and said, "Go get her, Czar!"

Wind ruffling his thick blond and white coat, Czar leaped from the porch and raced toward Kayla.

Kayla's heart felt like it was turning over and over, but she stood her ground. "You're my protection, Father in Heaven," she whispered. Czar stopped inches from her and growled menacingly. She could smell his breath and see his pointed teeth. Still Kayla didn't move or speak.

"Bring her to me, Czar," called Pansy in her raspy voice.

Czar bit Kayla's skirt and tugged.

Kayla's legs trembled, but she forced them to be steady as she walked to Pansy Butler. Close up, Kayla could see the deep wrinkles in Pansy's leather-tan face and her piercing blue eyes.

Pansy finally lowered the rifle and patted Czar's head. "Good boy."

Czar let go of Kayla and sank down on the porch, his paws on his front legs, his bushy tail swishing on the floor.

Kayla felt like a giant next to the old woman. She stood almost head and shoulders taller than Pansy.

Pansy peered up at Kayla. "I can't see like I once could. Come inside and read something for me." She reached for the doorknob, then shot a look over her shoulder at Kayla. "And you better be able to read!"

"I'll gladly read to you," said Kayla as she followed Pansy into the cluttered kitchen, then on to the front room that was just as cluttered. The house was too warm and smelled of camphor oil.

"Sit right there where the good light is," said Pansy, pushing Kayla toward a dark-green overstuffed chair in front of a tall, narrow window with a dirty cream-colored curtain hanging limply over it. Pansy pulled an old red leather-bound book from a shelf of books. She opened it carefully and held it out to Kayla. "And don't mumble when you read!"

Kayla looked at the yellowed pages. It was a world history book, and Pansy had opened it to the chapter on the czars of Russia. Kayla read the entire chapter before Pansy would let her quit.

Pansy leaned back in her rocker with her hands on her heart. "My papa came here from Russia. Couldn't speak a word of English. He married an American girl and settled down in Ohio and raised mules." It was almost as if Pansy were reciting her own history. "When I was ten years old we moved to Iowa, then on to Nebraska when I was fifteen. Papa died a year after I was married. But I learned all he knew about mules, and I taught it to Rachel." Pansy scowled. "Abel Larsen don't know beans about mules!"

Kayla closed the book and held it carefully in her lap. She could tell Pansy wanted to talk, just like Grandma had back in County Offaly. Kayla listened without interrupting. When Pansy finally seemed to be talked out Kayla said, "You tell me what chores you want done and I'll get right to them."

Pansy bristled. "I can do my own chores."

"I'd be happy to work together with you."

Pansy eased herself up. "Follow me then. And don't think you know more than me about my own chores. When Rachel comes over, she won't let me lift a finger. Makes me mad clear through. Does she think I'm an old lady ready for the grave? I'm not!"

Kayla helped clean out the chicken house, milked the cow, and cleaned out the stalls where Pansy kept her team of mules that pulled her buggy. While they worked, Kayla answered Pansy's questions about who she was. Indoors Kayla did the best she could to clean around the clutter, fixed a meal of chicken soup, then talked Pansy into letting her wash and trim her hair.

"You're a real handy one to have around," said Pansy as she admired her hair in the small looking glass on her dresser. Czar stayed close at her side. "How do you get along with Rachel's kids?"

"Just fine."

"Abel?"

"All right."

Pansy shook her head. "That's hard to believe."

"Come visit sometime and you'll see."

Pansy wrinkled her small nose. "Nobody there wants me."

"Why would you say that?"

Pansy sank to the edge of her bed and rested her hands on the faded patchwork quilt. Czar sprang up onto the foot of the bed and lay with his head on his paws. "Them kids are all scared spitless of me."

Kayla perched on the edge of a short armless rocker. "Why are they afraid of you? You're their grandma."

Pansy waved her hand in disgust. "They're worthless . . . the lot of 'em! Can't read or write. Don't have the backbone of a jellyfish."

"They are shy."

"Shy my hind foot! They're slow-witted."

"They don't seem to be."

"They are."

Kayla narrowed her eyes thoughtfully. "I could teach them to read and write."

"Ha!"

"I could. Do you have a few books I could borrow?"

"Rachel's got all the books you'd need. Ask her. She'll laugh at you too." Pansy rested her hand on Czar's head. "Then again, anybody that knows about the czars of Russia might be able to teach them kids readin' and writin'. Give it a shot. What can it hurt?"

"I'll be going back now," said Kayla as she stood.

"Back to Bitter Creek Ranch," said Pansy gruffly.

"Bitter Creek Ranch?" The name seemed to fit Rachel and Abel. Kayla didn't like that a bit.

"It's called that for the creek that runs through it. Indians named it years ago for a battle they had there. Both sides lost many lives. From that time on they called the creek Bitter Creek." Pansy fingered Czar's ears. "Rachel named the ranch when she moved there." Pansy's voice faded away, and she looked sad. "She was naming her own feelings."

"That's very sad," said Kayla.

"We made a mistake . . . Tooky and me did. Tooky was my husband, Rachel's papa. We made a real bad mistake." Pansy pushed herself up and scowled at Kayla. "But that's no business of yours, so don't pump me for information." Pansy waved her hand. "Get going, but be sure to come back. Tell Rachel I want you to come here regular."

"I will. You might like to meet my brother Timothy too."

"Can he read?"

"Yes . . . and write. He has a gift of gab too."

"I might want him to come . . . I might."

A few minutes later Kayla said good-bye and walked back across the prairie toward the Larsens'. It was later than she'd thought, and the wind had turned chilly. Ula had showed Kayla how to find her way back by the shape of the hills and a faint trail through the grass. She smiled as she thought of Pansy Butler. "She's just hungry for books and conversation, something the Larsens don't know about," said Kayla. Her voice seemed lost in the wide open spaces with the wind blowing tumbleweeds across the prairie like the boys in New York City rolled marbles.

When she was about halfway back she saw a movement to her left. She frowned and stopped in her tracks. Was it a coyote or a wolf out in broad daylight? Then she caught a glimpse of something blue. Was someone hiding to jump out at her? Maybe the person who was after Sterling? Her heart thudded against her rib cage, and her mouth felt bone-dry. Should she check it out? Maybe someone was lying hurt in the tall grass.

"Thank You, Father, for the angels watching over me," whispered Kayla as she slowly walked toward the blue object. She caught a flash of red, then heard a groan. Her muscles gathered, ready to leap away if someone jumped out at her.

Ducks flew across the sky, quacking loudly as they headed south for the winter.

Kayla walked closer and finally saw a man with bright red hair huddled in the grass. "Hello," said Kayla hesitantly.

The man looked up, and Kayla saw he was a boy older than herself. He wore a black suit, white shirt and collar, and a black tie. He looked like he'd come from New York City. He awkwardly stood up. He was tall with broad shoulders, narrow hips, and brown eyes full of pain. "How do you do," he said very politely.

"Do you need help?" she asked, still ready to spring away if he made a quick move.

"I certainly do," he said. "I don't know where I am."

"Nebraska."

He nodded, then groaned and gingerly touched his head. "I know that much . . . but where?" He spread his hand and waved his arm in a wide arc.

"The Larsens live about a half-mile that way, and Pansy Butler lives a half-mile back there."

"I don't know either."

"Who are you?"

He frowned slightly. "Boon Russell. And you?"

"Kayla O'Brian."

"Fresh from Ireland, sounds like."

She nodded. "Where is it you're from?"

He frowned in thought. "Vermont. I came by train to Nebraska." He rubbed his head again. "I hired a buggy in North Platte, but that's the last I remember."

"If I were still in New York City I'd say you've been tumbled and robbed. Did you check your purse?"

He touched his pockets, then gasped, "I have been robbed! Even my watch!"

"I'll be taking you to the Larsens' ranch where you can spend the night. Dark is falling, and we must be on our way." A tinge of doubt about taking him with her wriggled inside her. What if he was the thief who was after Sterling? Impatiently she pushed the thought aside. He did need help, and she wasn't about to leave him on his own in the middle of the prairie at night.

"I'm afraid I can't walk very fast . . . I feel weak and dizzy."

"Then I'll be walking slow beside you. 'Tis not safe for you to be out here alone."

He smiled into her eyes, and her pulse jumped strangely. "You're an angel of mercy, Kayla O'Brian."

"Thank you, Boon Russell." His kind words wrapped around her heart. With a smile she fell into step beside him. As tall as she was, he was taller. He stumbled, and she caught his arm. Her nerve ends tingled, and she jerked her hand away.

"Is something wrong?" he asked.

"No," she said through a dry throat. What was wrong with her? She wasn't one to lose her heart over a young man whose hair was as bright as a heart on a Valentine's Day card.

"Why would someone steal my things and dump me out in the middle of nowhere?"

"That's a good question."

"I mean to find the answer," he said grimly.

Kayla looked up at Boon. "I'll be helping you."

He smiled, and her heart took another strange dive.

The Tenderfoot

Boon Russell moaned again, and Kayla glanced at him in great concern. They were almost to the ranch, but the last several yards he'd slowed almost to a crawl. "Are you in terrible pain?" asked Kayla.

Boon lifted his head a fraction. His face was white. "I don't know if I can make it."

"You must!"

"My head's spinning like a top."

"Put your arm around my shoulders and lean on me." She caught his arm, forced her heart to stop leaping at the slightest touch from him, and put his arm around her shoulders. She slipped her arm around his waist and felt him put his weight on her. She smelled the wool of his jacket. She turned her head, and her cheek brushed the back of his hand. Against her will her pulse jumped. How could her emotions run rampant at such a time?

With great effort she turned her thoughts away from herself and back to Boon. "It's not much further. Please, keep trying. Don't think about how much your head aches or how dizzy you are. Think about the cup of cold water you'll be drinking, the warm house, and the fine supper you'll be eating."

"I'll try," Boon whispered.

Kayla made herself think of the same things instead of the young man walking with his arm around her. She helped him past the corral and the shed and onto the porch. She felt him sway, and her heart sank again. "We're almost there," she said.

She opened the door, and warm air along with smells of supper rushed out. She stepped inside with him, and all the family turned to stare at her, much like that morning when she'd first walked in. "This is Boon Russell," she said brightly.

Timothy pushed away from the table and ran to her side. "I was much worried about you, Kayla." Timothy took Boon's other side, and they eased him down onto Timothy's chair.

"Where'd you pick up this tenderfoot?" asked Abel with an angry shake of his head.

"Between here and Pansy Butler's place," said Kayla as she loosened Boon's tie and collar. "He was struck down and robbed."

"He can't stay here," said Rachel coldly as she lifted her cup of steaming coffee.

"I can't be hearing right!" Wide-eyed, Kayla stared at Rachel. "You couldn't be putting the poor soul out on his ear."

"I can and I will," said Rachel.

Kayla turned from Rachel in shock and once again wondered if she and Timothy had made a grave mistake in agreeing to be taken in by Rachel Larsen. Timothy had known Rachel would be taking them even before Rachel had spoken for them at the Orphan Train. Timothy had a way of knowing things just like Mama had. This time maybe Timothy's knowing was mistaken!

"Get him out of here now," snapped Rachel.

"And just where will he go, Rachel?" asked Abel with a frown.

"Not here," she said.

"We can't be sending him out on his own in this condition," said Kayla. Red circles spotted her cheeks, and she spoke with great determination. "Greene, please give me a hand to carry him upstairs."

Greene blushed and started to stand, but Rachel waved him back down.

Her blue eyes smoldering, Rachel slowly stood and walked around to Kayla. "There is only one boss in this house, Kayla O'Brian, and it's me."

Kayla flushed. "I am quite sorry for stepping out of bounds, Rachel. But Boon needs a helping hand. You wouldn't be denying him that now, would you?"

"I already have," said Rachel coldly.

Abel rapped the table with his fists and made his silverware jump. All eyes turned on him. "I am the boss in this house, Rachel Larsen. You like to forget that. I say we take the boy upstairs and see what we can do for him . . . And what I say goes."

Rachel's jaw tightened as she glared at Abel. Finally she grabbed her hat and coat and hurried out the door, slamming it loudly.

"Greene, help Kayla," said Abel wearily. "The rest of you kids finish supper and get this mess cleaned up."

"I'll save a plate for you, Kayla," said Ula softly.

"Thanks," said Kayla, smiling at Ula. "I'll try to get Boon to eat something too."

Greene lifted Boon and with straining muscles carried him upstairs to the boys' room.

Kayla pulled back the quilt and blanket that she and Ula had spread in place that morning, and Greene carefully laid Boon down.

"Thanks, Greene."

Greene flushed and ducked his head. His tangled black hair hung over his forehead and down to his collar. His dirty gray long johns showed at the rolled-up cuffs and neck of his blue plaid shirt.

"I'll need you to help take off his boots and jacket."

Greene pulled off Boon's black riding boots and black socks and dropped them with a clatter on the plank floor. He eased off Boon's jacket, and Kayla took off his tie and collar.

"Did he get hit in the head?" asked Greene.

Kayla jumped in surprise to hear Greene speak. "Yes . . . He has a lump right here." Kayla showed Greene the lump and watched as Greene gently ran his fingers over it, then parted Boon's red hair and studied it.

Greene stepped away from the bed, but didn't look at Kayla. "He is a tenderfoot, but he needs help."

"And what is a tenderfoot?" asked Kayla with a slight frown.

"A person from the city who doesn't know his way around a ranch."

"And are Timothy and I tenderfeet?"

Greene shook his head, his eyes down. "I thought you were, but you're not."

"Thank you," said Kayla with a low chuckle.

"I'll fill the India rubber bottle with cold water right from the well and put it on the swelling. Give him a drink of water and let him sleep. He should be fine by tomorrow."

Kayla smiled. "Greene, 'tis a doctor you should be!"

He beamed with pleasure, then scowled. "That'll never happen."

"And why not? You live in America. You can do anything, be anything you want!"

Greene lifted haggard eyes to Kayla. "Not always." He turned and walked to the door. "I'll send Scott up with a cup of water." He walked out of the room, his steps heavy.

Kayla frowned thoughtfully after him, then turned to look down at Boon. His eyes were closed, but she knew he wasn't sleeping. "You're in good hands, Boon Russell." She gently rubbed back the thick red hair on his wide forehead. "Heavenly Father, fill Boon with Your love and peace. Jesus, thank You for Your healing power. Help us to take good care of Boon, and help him to find his way home again."

Boon moaned and opened his eyes. They were filled with despair. "I can . . . never go . . . home," he whispered.

"But why?"

"I . . . killed . . . a man."

Kayla gasped and pressed her hand to her mouth. Was he out of his head? "You can't be meaning it, Boon," she whispered.

"My . . . grandpa," he said hoarsely.

Kayla's stomach knotted, and for once she was at a lack for words.

Just then Scott ran in with a cup of water. Kayla thanked him and helped Boon drink it. She handed the empty cup to Scott, and he ran back out with it as Greene walked in with the India rubber bottle of cold water. He propped it so it was against the lump on Boon's head.

Kayla leaned down to Boon and whispered, "We'll take care of you, Boon. You rest now."

"Thank you, Kayla O'Brian," whispered Boon weakly.

She nodded, then stepped away from the bed. "Greene, I'll be leaving now. You undress Boon so he can sleep in comfort."

"You were brave to bring him home," said Greene.

Kayla nodded stiffly. Was Boon really a killer, or was his mind wandering? "I couldn't leave him all alone and hurt."

"I'm glad." Greene's blue eyes softened. "You saved the pup Ma shot. I'm glad about that too. The girls named her Brownie." For the first time Greene smiled.

Kayla smiled at him, said good night to Boon, and walked out of the room. She stopped at the top of the stairs and leaned her head against the plastered wall. "Heavenly Father, I thought 'twas a mistake Timothy and me coming here, but I was wrong. You sent us here as Your light in this dark household. Help us show Your great love to this sad family . . . and to Boon Russell."

Kayla bit her bottom lip. What if Boon Russell was another Billy the Kid, the terrible killer all the orphans had talked about since they'd crossed the Missouri River? Maybe she'd brought danger into the Larsen family just because her silly heart wouldn't let her leave him on the prairie for the wild animals.

Timothy stopped at the bottom of the stairs. "Kayla . . ." he said softly. He saw her turmoil, and he wanted to help. "Don't let what Rachel said make you feel bad."

Kayla walked slowly down the steps, her hand on the wall for support. She gripped Timothy's hand. "I could not leave him out in the wilds alone!"

"And 'tis a good thing you couldn't! You are an O'Brian!"

Kayla laughed and hugged Timothy hard. "But what of Rachel?"

"She has a great sadness inside her, Kayla. Her anger came from that sadness, not from you bringing home Boon Russell."

"'Tis true, Timothy." Kayla nodded. "But her words hurt me deep."

"You're bigger than that, Kayla! You're an O'Brian."

Kayla laughed and jabbed Timothy's arm. "It is me that's always saying it to you."

He grinned. "I know. I saw a chance to get back at you." He tugged on her hand. "Come eat supper."

She squeezed his hand and walked to the kitchen. Somehow she'd find a way to help Rachel Larsen.

A Talk with Rachel

Shivering in the cold, Kayla tugged her coat tighter around her thin body and stopped just outside the barn. Moonlight was bright enough to cast a shadow. Stars filled the sky and seemed low enough to touch. A week had passed since she'd brought Boon to Bitter Creek Ranch. And a week had passed since Rachel had spoken to her.

A mare nickered, and the donkey brayed, then all was quiet. Kayla whispered, "You're my strength and my help, Father God." Kayla squared her shoulders and pushed open the barn door.

Rachel sat with her back against Sterling's stall, the lantern above her, a book in her hand. She looked up, frowned, and went back to reading.

Trembling, Kayla closed the door. The pungent odor stung her nose. Sterling moved restlessly. Kayla nervously fingered the button on her coat. She would not back down just because Rachel wasn't speaking to her! "I came to guard Sterling so you could sleep in your own bed tonight."

Rachel snapped her book closed. "And was this Abel's idea?"

Kayla frowned "No . . . my own."

Rachel looked surprised, then quickly masked it. "Go back to the house."

"I am keeping watch tonight," said Kayla as she reached for a blanket from the shelf. Jane had given her long underwear to put on under her clothes. They felt strange but warm.

"Do what you please. It seems you do anyway."

Kayla ignored that, even though it hurt her feelings. "Boon is well enough to leave," said Kayla with a slight catch in her voice. She hated to think of him going, but maybe when he did some of the tension would go with him.

"I reckon that means one of us has to take time out to drive him to town."

Kayla nodded.

"Then he'll have to wait until we need to go in for supplies." Rachel opened her book and went back to reading.

Kayla leaned against the stall and patted Sterling's neck. "Greene said the buyer is coming in a few days for Sterling."

Rachel kept on reading.

Kayla wrapped the blanket around her shoulders and sat down beside Rachel.

After a long time Rachel said, "There's no reason for two of us to stay out here."

"It's me that'll be staying," said Kayla. "You've been out here every night for a week."

"Didn't your mother teach you to obey?"

Kayla blinked back sudden tears. "That she did. But she taught me to help others too."

"And was she as stubborn as you are?"

"She and Papa both." Kayla smiled. "Papa could outstubborn Mama. But, oh, they loved each other! 'Twas grand to see the love between them."

"Much like the love between Abel and me," said Rachel bitterly.

Kayla saw the pain in Rachel's eyes. "Your mother told me about the two of you."

Rachel gasped as she stared in shock at Kayla. "How dare she! She had no right!"

"I asked her why you were so sad."

"Sad!" Rachel jumped up, and the book and blanket fell to the dirt floor. "Why would you think I'm sad?"

"Your eyes say so."

Rachel threw up her arms. "Why did I ever bring the two of you here? I almost left when I couldn't find a big strong boy like Abel wanted, but I didn't. Why?"

Kayla let her blanket fall as she stood. "God loves you, Rachel Larsen. He sent us here to help you."

Rachel spun on her heels, grabbed her rifle, and ran from the barn.

Sighing, Kayla wrapped both blankets around her shoulders and sat back down. She picked up Rachel's book. It was one Kayla had not read before, written by Mark Twain, an author she'd never heard of. She started reading and soon became absorbed in Tom Sawyer's story. After a while her eyelids drooped, and she knew she had to stop reading no matter how badly she wanted to keep on. She'd read history to Pansy Butler every day the past week, but this was an adventure story that gripped her. Reluctantly she carefully set the book aside, turned out the lantern, and curled against Sterling's stall. The night sounds faded away, and she slept.

When she woke she felt almost smothered in the blankets. She tried to pull her arm free to flip the blanket off her face, but she couldn't move her arm. She jerked her head, but still the blanket wouldn't move. The blanket suddenly felt too rough and too hot. She jerked harder at her arms, but she couldn't get them free of the blanket. She kicked and found she couldn't move one leg without the other. Her heart sank. She wasn't just tangled in her blankets — she was tied up!

"Sterling!" she cried, but the cry was muffled against the rough wool blanket.

Just then Timothy walked into the barn to see why Kayla wasn't on time for breakfast. He saw the rolled-up blankets tied with a rope and Sterling's empty stall. "Kayla!" he cried, running to her side.

She heard his voice, and tears of frustration burned her eyes. "Timothy! Get me out of this!"

Timothy quickly released Kayla, and she leaped up, her mass of black hair wild around her head and shoulders. Her face was blotchy red.

"How could I let someone steal Sterling?" she cried, gripping the door of the stall.

"Are you hurt, Kayla?" asked Timothy in concern.

She frowned as she checked herself over. "I don't feel like it." Her face hardened. "But embarrassed I am! Timothy, how could I let such a terrible thing happen? Someone took Sterling! Walked in here and took Sterling right beneath my nose!"

Timothy patted Kayla's arm, but she brushed him aside. "We have to go tell," he said.

Kayla gasped. "Tell? Oh, Rachel will be booting us out for sure!" Kayla pressed her hands to her flushed cheeks and wouldn't listen to the words of comfort Timothy tried to give her. "And well I deserve it too! But not you, Timothy. You don't deserve to be booted out. Me! I don't deserve even to be an O'Brian!" She sank to the floor and burst into tears.

"Kayla, don't cry."

She cried harder, her face buried in her hands.

Timothy tried to calm her, but finally gave up and ran to the house. He stopped at the door and took a deep breath. His hand shook as he turned the knob and pushed the door open. Smells of bacon and coffee hit him as he stepped into the warm kitchen. "Rachel, I need you to come with me to the barn," he said hoarsely.

"I'm eating," she said.

Abel's brows shot almost to his hairline. "What's wrong?"

Butterflies fluttered in Timothy's stomach, but he managed to say, "Somebody took Sterling."

Rachel jumped up, spilling her cup of coffee. "Sterling?"

"Greene, help me to the barn," cried Abel, struggling to stand.

"Is Kayla hurt?" asked Boon in alarm.

"No," said Timothy as he ran out with Rachel close behind and the others following.

In the barn Rachel ran right to Sterling's stall as if she'd find the answer to where he'd gone.

Kayla struggled to control her sobs as she stood beside Rachel. "I don't deserve your forgiveness for this," she whispered hoarsely.

"No, you don't," said Rachel coldly.

Kayla bit her lip and groaned.

As the others crowded around the stall, Rachel ran to the door and looked for tracks.

"See anything?" asked Abel as he leaned heavily on his cane and Greene.

Rachel turned to Abel, her face white. "It looks like they rubbed out the tracks with a branch!"

Kayla moaned.

"Are you hurt, Kayla?" asked Boon in a low voice.

Kayla turned away from him to hide her tears and her misery. "I'm not hurt," she said stiffly. "'Twould be better if I was!"

"Don't say that!" cried Ula, catching Kayla's coat sleeve. "I'm glad you're not hurt!"

Kayla pulled herself together enough to smile weakly at Ula. This was not the time to carry on and feel sorry for herself.

"They probably used knockout drops on her," said Boon. "It stands to reason, since she didn't hear anything or wake up when they rolled her in the blankets and tied her up."

"Knockout drops?" whispered Kayla, trembling.

"That makes sense," said Greene.

Abel thumped his cane. "We got to find Sterling and get him back here before the buyer comes."

"*We?*" said Rachel with a sneer as she pointed at Abel's bad leg.

Color crept up Abel's neck and over his face.

"I'll go," said Greene.

"I can go with him," said Boon.

"And I'll go with the both of you," said Rachel grimly. "The rest of you get the chores done. Jane, do the best you can with the mules we've been working with."

"Yes, Ma," said Jane.

Kayla touched Rachel's arm. "Will you be booting us out?"

"I should . . . But I gave my word to take you in."

"And she never goes back on her word," said Abel bitterly.

Rachel glared at Abel and walked past him without another word.

Kayla plucked at Timothy's sleeve. "We'll be staying after all," she whispered.

Later, while Timothy and Scott fed the animals and Ula cleaned the kitchen, Kayla walked to the corral with Jane. "You show me what to do and I'll do it," Kayla said.

"Do you know anything about mules?" asked Jane as she climbed over the fence. She wore a blue linsey-woolsey dress patched in three places, cowboy boots, and an old hat much like Rachel's.

"My grandma had a mule, so I know some. And your grandma has been teaching me some." Kayla watched the mules standing in the middle of the corral. Suddenly she had an idea. "Jane, I'm going to drive over and get your grandma and bring her back to help you."

Jane cringed against the fence, her face ashen. "Don't, Kayla! She hates me."

"She won't once she sees what a fine girl you are and how much you know about mules." Kayla touched Jane's hand. "I have to do something for your mama. I can help her by bringing Pansy here to do what your mama would be doing if she wasn't out hunting for Sterling."

Jane sighed heavily "She *is* real good at training mules. You can get her. I'll help you hitch up the buggy."

"Thank you, Jane. When she gets here, you say hello to her and tell her thanks for coming. That'll make her feel wanted." Kayla hugged Jane, and Jane jerked back in surprise and embarrassment.

Several minutes later Kayla tied the team to the hitching post outside Pansy's back door. Pansy and Czar stood on the porch, waiting.

"Why'd you drive over?" asked Pansy suspiciously.

Kayla quickly told her, "They need your help, Pansy."

"Doing what?" asked Pansy, scowling.

"Training the mules with Jane. She's doing a fine job, but she needs help because Rachel went looking for Sterling. The buyers are coming soon, and they expect the mules to be ready."

Pansy looked down at Czar. "What d' you think, Czar? Shall we go?"

Czar waved his blond and white plume of a tail and whined.

Pansy pursed her lips thoughtfully, and Kayla stood quietly and waited. She knew this was not the time to beg. Finally Pansy pulled at her gunbelt, tugged her hat low on her forehead, and patted Czar's head. "Let's get a move on if we're going today," she said, walking around to climb in the buggy.

Kayla untied the line and ran around to the other side. They rode in silence to the ranch.

Czar leaped out of the buggy first, then Pansy followed. She looked around. "It's been a good long time since I been here."

Just then Jane stepped up to Pansy. "Hello, Grandma," she said. "Thanks for coming."

Pansy stared at Jane in surprise, then hiked up her gunbelt. "What else could I do with Kayla O'Brian here begging me?"

Kayla laughed. "Now, Pansy Butler, you know you came on your own accord. You wanted to help Jane."

Pansy chuckled. "Let's get to it."

Kayla waved Timothy and Scott over to unhitch the team, then she ran with Pansy and Jane to the corral.

Horses

On her return from taking Pansy home, Kayla slowly led the team of mules into the corral and watched them roll in the grass. Timothy had told her Rachel and the boys weren't back yet even though it was getting late.

"And 'tis all my fault," muttered Kayla as she walked slowly to the house. She stood on the porch, her head down, her shoulders drooping.

"Kayla!" shouted Scott, running as fast as his short, fat legs could carry him. "Horses are coming!"

She whirled around. "Horses?" She looked where Scott was pointing. A cloud of dust rose up from the ground, and a herd of horses was racing right toward the ranch. Wind caught the dust and flung it across the open prairie. The sound of pounding hooves grew louder. Shivers ran down Kayla's spine.

"They'll run us down!" shouted Scott as he sped to the house "Pa! Pa! Horses!"

Frantically Kayla looked around for Timothy and finally

spotted him near the sod chicken house. "Timothy, do you see them?" she called.

"That I do!" he yelled back, sounding excited. "And they're coming this way fast."

The door opened, and Abel stood there leaning heavily on his cane.

"But won't they stop before they reach us? Won't they turn away?" cried Kayla.

"They might not," said Abel. "Timothy, get up here fast!"

Jane and Ula strained to see around Abel. "Where's Brownie?" asked Ula in alarm.

"Brownie!" cried Scott as he ran down the long porch.

Kayla looked and finally spotted the overgrown pup digging at the side of the granary. "Brownie!" she called.

The pup kept digging.

"Timothy, get Brownie," shouted Abel.

"Brownie!" Timothy called as he ran toward him. Brownie lifted his head and dodged away from Timothy. "Come back here, Brownie!"

"Brownie! Brownie!" shouted Scott.

"He don't know his name yet," said Jane, sounding close to tears.

"Them horses will trample him into mush," said Scott, his face as gray as the dust cloud.

Suddenly Ula ducked under Abel's arm and dashed out after the pup. The pounding hooves of the horses made the ground tremble.

"Come back, Ula!" shouted Abel. He started to move and gasped in pain.

"Ula!" cried Jane. "Get her, Kayla!"

Kayla dashed after the little girl and finally caught her near the windmill. "We have to get to the house."

Ula jerked free. "I got to get Brownie!"

"She'll take care of herself." Kayla lunged forward and caught Ula's hand. "The horses are closer! Come on!" Sweat popped out on Kayla's face. She half-dragged Ula across the yard.

"I got to get Brownie," said Ula, sobbing hysterically as she struggled to get away from Kayla.

Kayla hung on even more tightly.

Across the yard Timothy leaped on Brownie. She snarled and snapped, but Timothy kept a firm grip on her. "Stop it, Brownie! I'm trying to help you." He carried her awkwardly to the shed and shut her inside. She barked and scratched at the door.

"Hurry, Timothy!" shouted Abel.

Timothy looked over his shoulder, and his blood ran cold. The horses were so close he could see the wild look in their eyes. Timothy raced to the house and leaped up on the porch just as the first horse reached the yard.

Kayla grabbed him and hugged him hard, then set him free to watch the horses race across the yard. They tore up chunks of grass and a couple of bushes that Rachel had been babying along, leaving behind a cloud of dust that choked Kayla.

No one on the porch spoke or moved.

Just then a horse screamed in terror and pain. Kayla saw that it had gone through the barbed-wire fence around the garden. Others in the herd followed, cutting themselves on the wire. Several others veered off and hit against the sod chicken house.

Finally all but one horse was gone. Its front legs were

caught in the barbed-wire. Struggling to get free, it screamed in agony. The terrible sound rolled across the prairie in the sudden silence after the pounding hooves.

"Pa, help it," begged Ula.

"There's nothing I can do," Abel said sharply. He slapped his leg and tried to walk on it, but almost fell. He caught himself and leaned heavily against a porch post.

"If that was a mule it would just stand there and not get cut more," said Jane in disgust. "Horses are so dumb!"

Timothy shot Jane an angry look. "Horses are grand animals! I'll take care of it." He started off the porch.

"Get back here!" snapped Abel. "That horse will kill you in its pain."

"What can we do?" asked Kayla. She couldn't stand to see the magnificent sorrel in such agony.

"Look! Here come some riders," said Scott, pointing.

Two of the riders stopped in the yard near the tangled sorrel, while the others thundered after the herd. One man wore a flowered vest over his gray shirt and a wide-brimmed gray hat. The other man wore a black hat and a black coat covered with dust. Kayla watched the man with the flowered vest uncoil his rope from the saddle horn and swing a wide loop. She glanced at the man in black to see him doing the same thing. That man roped the sorrel around the neck and the other around the back feet as the horse kicked out. They held the horse tight. The man in the flowered vest jumped off his horse with wire cutters in his hand. His mount held the rope taut. Quickly the man cut the horse free. Blood flowed down the sorrel's front legs, and the horse snorted and tried to buck, but it couldn't with the ropes holding him.

The man in the flowered vest walked to the porch. He

lifted his dusty wide-brimmed hat. "Fint Mathis here," he said.

"Abel Larsen," said Abel. "It looks like you had a bit of trouble."

Fint nodded. "I'm sure sorry about this. Some crazy man leadin' a white mule spooked 'em."

Kayla's pulse leaped.

"Will that horse die?" asked Ula in a faint voice.

"I reckon not." Fint looked at Abel. "Figure up the expenses . . . We'll make it right."

"Where'd you see the white mule?" asked Abel.

"Over near the Rhoba place," said Fint. "You interested in white mules?"

Kayla gripped her hands behind her back and could barely stand still.

Abel quickly told Fint about their mule being stolen. "Could be ours. We'll check into it. What's the man look like that had him?"

Fint shrugged. "I couldn't get too good a look, but he was big, had on overalls and a wore-out hat. Rode a brown mule."

Kayla wanted to ask Abel if he knew the man, but she forced back the words.

Timothy nudged her, and she glanced at him and nodded slightly.

While Abel and Fint talked, Ula whispered to Kayla, "I'll give that man some salve to put on the horse."

Kayla nodded, and Ula ran to the barn for the salve.

Finally Fint pushed his hat to the back of his head. "Name a fair price for this damage and I'll be glad to meet it."

Abel frowned thoughtfully. "How about three of your horses?"

Timothy sucked in his breath.

Kayla's eyes sparkled in anticipation.

Fint looped his thumbs around his gunbelt and finally nodded. "I'll have Rusty cut 'em out for you."

"My pick," said Abel.

Fint slowly shook his head. "Can't let you do that."

"I pick or the deal's off," said Abel gruffly.

"They're my horses and it's my say. Take it or leave it." Fint narrowed his dark eyes. "Take it or leave it," he repeated.

Kayla took a step forward. "You could let my little brother pick." She stressed the word *little*.

Abel scowled at Kayla. "I want to pick 'em myself. It's not a kid's job."

Fint laughed and slapped his thigh. Dust billowed out. "I say we let the kid pick. It'll be fair to both of us."

Abel's jaw tightened, but he finally agreed.

Timothy's stomach flip-flopped, and he could hardly stand still. He grinned at Kayla, and she grinned back.

Several minutes later the riders returned with a quiet herd of dust-covered horses. While they drank at Bitter Creek Timothy walked among them, looking them over just as Papa had trained him to do.

Her icy hands locked in front of her, Kayla stood beside Fint and Abel, who leaned heavily on his cane. He'd managed to walk to the creek by himself though. The men talked, but Kayla was too engrossed in watching Timothy to listen. Night was falling, and she thought it might be too dark for Timothy to see.

At last Timothy chose a young sorrel stallion, a bay filly, and a chestnut mare.

Fint frowned. "I think I been had," he said as his men

led the horses to the barn to put them in stalls for the night. "That kid picked some of my best stock."

Kayla beamed with pride.

Abel pointed to a tall gray gelding. "I'd have chosen that one."

Kayla looked at the gelding, and she knew Timothy had passed him by because of the wild look in his eye.

"He's a fine-lookin' piece of horse flesh," said Fint, "but he's got a wild side to him. I'm thinkin' strong of sellin' him to the Wild West Show. He bucks even my best riders off."

Abel shot a puzzled look at Kayla before he turned back to Fint. "I reckon I'm lucky I didn't get to pick."

"Why would you want a stallion on a mule ranch?" asked Fint.

Abel shrugged. "A man can raise both mules and horses."

"I reckon so," said Fint.

Kayla felt a bubble of excitement burst in her.

"We'll be ridin' out now," said Fint. "There's gonna be a full moon again tonight, so I'll push 'til I get to my place." He shook Abel's hand. "Sure sorry about tearin' your place up."

"It can be fixed," said Abel.

"Head 'em up, boys!" called Fint as he walked to his horse.

Kayla watched Fint mount and ride away. She laughed softly. She and Timothy would be having horses to train after all!

Abel turned to Kayla, his eyes thoughtful. "Did Timothy pick out those horses by accident?"

She laughed. "'Twas no accident, Abel Larsen. My Timothy knows horses."

Abel grinned, then tipped back his head and laughed. The laughter rolled out of Abel as if had been locked inside for a very long time. It sounded good to Kayla.

She ran to catch up with Timothy on his way to the barn. Inside she looked the horses over carefully. "Fint said you chose some of his best," said Kayla proudly.

"I know," said Timothy as he leaned against the stall door and studied the filly. "There were a couple of others I wanted, but I knew these three were right for us."

They talked a while about the horses, then Kayla said, "I was that glad to hear about the white mule."

"If Rachel doesn't find Sterling today, maybe we can ride over to the Rhoba place in the morning and check on that white mule," said Timothy.

Kayla laughed softly. "I was thinking the same thing."

"I know." Timothy grinned and jabbed Kayla's arm.

Just then Rachel stormed into the barn, her face dark with anger. Greene stopped right behind her. "Just what went on here?" she asked.

Kayla started to answer, but Abel cut her off. He leaned heavily on his cane as he walked into the barn.

Rachel turned slowly and stared at him. "Decided you could walk, did you?"

"I decided I could endure the pain," he said gruffly. "You kids get to the house and let me talk to Rachel alone."

As Kayla walked outdoors beside Timothy and Greene, she saw the startled look on Rachel's face.

"Did you find Sterling?" Timothy asked.

Greene shook his head.

"Where's Boon?" asked Kayla with a quick look around. It was almost too dark to see.

Greene tugged at his hat brim. "Ma left him in town."

Kayla gasped.

"She said since we were there, Boon might as well stay and get on with his own plans."

Tears burned Kayla's eyes, but she forced them back. "Did he say anything?"

"Like what?" asked Greene.

"Like good-bye to me?" she whispered.

Greene shrugged. "Not that I heard."

Timothy touched Kayla's arm. "We could ride in and try to see him before he goes back east."

"Ma won't let you," said Greene.

"Why not?" asked Kayla in alarm.

"She picked up supplies while we were in town, so there's no reason to go again for a good long time."

Kayla looked back toward the barn, her jaw tight. She'd tried hard to be kind and forgiving, but no more! Not after this. "I hate her," she said under her breath. The ugly words stabbed into her heart, but she wouldn't take them back.

Abel's Announcement

Kayla sank heavily on her chair at the breakfast table. She didn't feel like eating now or ever.

"Are you sick?" whispered Timothy for her ears alone while the others all sat quietly in their places.

She shook her head.

"Kayla, you can thank God for the food," said Abel.

She stiffened.

"Can I do it this morning?" asked Timothy because he knew how Kayla felt.

Abel nodded and bowed his head.

"Heavenly Father, 'tis a grand day You've given us. Thank You for this fine food and for all of Your blessings to us, especially the three magnificent horses. Help us find Sterling. And help us to be kind and loving to each other. In Jesus' name, Amen."

Rachel snorted and clicked her spoon in her cup as she stirred sugar in her coffee.

After they'd eaten a while Abel said, "Ula, how is Brownie this morning?"

All eyes turned in shock to Abel. Ula flushed to the roots of her brown braids. She looked quickly at Rachel, who kept on eating as if she hadn't heard Abel.

Finally Ula said, "Brownie ate all her food and didn't growl once at me."

"Good," said Abel. He chewed a bite of biscuit and swallowed a sip of coffee.

Kayla saw the empty spot where Boon had sat the past week, and she couldn't eat another bite. He'd told her about the buggy accident that had caused his grandpa's death. He'd been showing off and driving too fast, and the buggy had tipped over, pinning his grandpa under it. Boon had left home just after the funeral, vowing never to return. She had convinced him to go home to see his parents because they were sure to miss him and be worried about him. He'd told her she was a wonderful girl and that he'd never forget her even if he stayed home. But he probably would miss her, especially now that he was gone before she could tell him she wanted him to write to her and that she'd write back.

Timothy nudged her, and she jumped. "Abel wants to know if you and me will go check on Sterling at the Rhoba place."

She wanted to refuse, but she nodded. It would be good to be as far away from Rachel as she could get.

"You kids check the place over, and if you see Sterling, come tell me. Don't try anything on your own. We don't want you getting hurt."

"I'll go with them," said Greene.

"You have work here," snapped Rachel. "We got a lot to catch up on since we were gone all day yesterday." She shot a look at Kayla, and Kayla cringed.

Abel cleared his throat. "I have something I want to say." He looked right at Rachel. She wouldn't look at him.

Kayla found her interest caught even though she was still angry at Rachel because Boon was gone. Kayla noticed the other kids were interested too.

Abel leaned back in his chair and rested his hands lightly on his legs. He had shaved and combed his hair. "From now on I assign the work for the day. Your ma needs a rest."

Rachel dropped her fork to her plate with a clatter.

"You need a rest, Rachel," said Abel firmly. He looked around the table. "Greene, you go do Pansy's chores today."

Greene sank back, his face pale.

"Jane, you do the best you can working with the mules. Your grandma said she'd come over again to help you."

"What?" Rachel looked at Abel as if he'd gone crazy. "Mama wouldn't set her foot on this place."

"She came yesterday," said Abel. "She worked with Jane . . . and did a good job of it too, even if she is old."

"And how did that come about?" asked Rachel, looking right at Kayla.

"I brought her over," said Kayla coldly.

"I might've known," muttered Rachel.

"What about me, Pa?" asked Scott.

"You'll herd the mules from the back corral out onto the prairie. Keep a close watch, and keep 'em tight together just in case."

"In case of what?" asked Timothy.

"In case someone wants more than just Sterling," said Abel grimly.

Timothy nodded, determined more than ever to find the man who'd taken Sterling.

"Ula, you'll clean the house," said Abel. "When you're done you can train Brownie."

Ula smiled.

"And just what will I be doing all day?" asked Rachel coldly.

Abel leaned forward with a smile. "You will sit in the rocker and read your book."

Rachel's mouth fell open. She snapped it closed, then said, "That's ridiculous!"

Kayla locked her hands in her lap. Why was Abel being so nice to Rachel? She didn't deserve kindness or friendship or love.

Abel shrugged. "Yesterday I laughed, Rachel . . . A real belly laugh. And all my anger and bitterness rolled right out with that laugh. Yesterday Timothy chose three fine horses for us. Horses! We are no longer just a mule ranch, but we now will deal in horses and in mules, something I've wanted to do for years."

A muscle jumped in Rachel's jaw.

Timothy reached over and secretly squeezed Kayla's hand.

Kayla tried to squeeze his hand back, but she couldn't.

Abel leaned his elbows on the table and laced his fingers together. "Kayla reminded me the other day that I'm the head of the house. It ate away at me. But yesterday I swore I'd start acting like the head of this house. So, Rachel, today you're taking a day-long rest. Tomorrow you can work again."

A strange look crossed Rachel's face, but then she masked it with her usual hard look. She brushed a loose strand of hair off her cheek that had come free from the bun at the nape of her neck. She pushed back her chair and walked to the front room.

"I never saw Ma rest before," whispered Scott, his eyes big in his round face.

"You will from now on," said Abel with a firm nod. He pushed back his chair, grimaced with pain, then stood. "I'm going to check on our horses. Coming, Timothy?"

"That I am!" Timothy jumped up with a glad laugh.

When Kayla walked into the barn several minutes later, Abel was leaning on the stall door and looking at the mare. Timothy was outside. "Abel . . ." she said hesitantly.

He glanced around. "Why the long face, Kayla?"

She hesitated, then told him about Rachel leaving Boon in town. "So . . . is there a way I could be seeing Boon to say good-bye?"

Abel twisted around, careful of his bad leg. "I'll give it some thought, Kayla. You deserve to go to town to see Boon. It's just that I don't know if you can get there before he leaves."

Kayla's anger toward Rachel burned even hotter.

"You're the girl who believes in miracles," said Abel. "Pray that Boon will hang around long enough for you to see him."

Kayla barely nodded. Right now she was too angry to pray. "I'll be riding with Timothy over to the Rhoba place," she said in a low, tight voice.

"I told Timothy the way," said Abel. "You two be careful."

Kayla nodded and walked out to where Timothy was waiting with two of the brood mares saddled and waiting. A warm breeze blew a tumbleweed across the yard. A rooster crowed from the top rail of the fence.

"I told Abel it wouldn't be fitting for us to be riding mules," said Timothy with a twinkle in his blue eyes.

Kayla gripped the saddle horn, but couldn't find the strength to mount.

"'Tis the anger in your heart that's hurting you, Kayla O'Brian," said Timothy softly.

"I know."

"You best be ridding yourself of it."

"I can't."

"You can! You are an O'Brian!" Timothy's voice rang out. "The great God of the universe dwells in you! His strength is yours for the taking!"

"I can't," she whispered.

"You have no choice, Kayla O'Brian!"

She turned to him, her eyes flashing.

Timothy almost backed down, but he squared his shoulders. "Papa showed us in the Scriptures that we are to put away such anger, for your anger does not bring about the righteous life that God desires."

"I don't care," whispered Kayla brokenly.

"You care, Kayla O'Brian."

She shook her head.

"And you must put away your anger!"

Again she shook her head.

"You must obey!"

She trembled.

"An O'Brian obeys."

Great tears welled up in Kayla's eyes, and finally she nodded. "You are right." She covered her face with trembling hands. "I now put away my anger at Rachel Larsen. With God's help I . . . forgive . . . her." The heavy weight that had been pressing down on Kayla melted away. "Thank You, Jesus." She lifted her head and smiled.

"Let's go check out the Rhoba place," said Timothy as he sprang into the saddle.

Suddenly the day seemed full of promise to Kayla. She reached through her legs for the back tail of her dress, pulled it forward and up, and tucked it in the belt around her narrow waist. She stepped into the stirrup and swung her leg over the saddle. "Timothy, 'tis good to be riding again!"

The Rhoba Place

Kayla stopped her mare beside Timothy's and looked at the wide valley that led to the Rhoba place. The buildings were all made of sod. Greene had told them many people built sod buildings because wood was so scarce in Nebraska. The sod was like giant bricks cut from the ground with a plow, then stacked on each other with the grassy side out and the roots in. Kayla shuddered as she thought of the bugs, mice, and snakes that could crawl right through the walls into the house.

Cattle wandered around a windmill, making the spot beside the big tank muddy. A big black dog that looked like a wolf stood at the side of the sod house barking at them. A woman stepped outside the house, shielded her eyes with her hand, and looked in the direction the dog was barking.

Timothy lifted his arm in a wave, and the woman did the same. "Abel said four people live here — Mazie and Tooker and their kids Korey and Pearl. They're from Missouri. That must be Mazie Rhoba."

"I wonder if they have Sterling." The warm wind blew

Kayla's hair that hung below her bonnet. A flock of geese flew overhead, honking loudly.

"We'll know soon," said Timothy, urging his mare forward.

"Thank You, Father God, for Your help," whispered Kayla as she nudged her mare with her knees.

They rode down the long hill and across the wide valley and stopped near the woman. Up close Kayla saw her tired eyes and too-thin body. She had a corncob pipe in her drooping mouth.

"Hello," said Kayla.

"We're Timothy and Kayla O'Brian," said Timothy.

"Climb down and set a spell," said the woman. "I be Mazie Rhoba." She pulled the pipe from her mouth and shouted, "Korey, get yerself out here! We got company. Bring Pearl with you."

Kayla dropped to the ground and tied the reins around the hitching rail, and Timothy did the same. The big dog sniffed her, then Timothy.

Korey walked out, his hand curled around Pearl's arm. Pearl was about Jane's age but walked with a bad limp. She had tangled brown hair, bloodshot eyes, and a withered arm; drool ran from the corner of her mouth. Korey was tall and wide and wore bibbed overalls and a floppy hat. He could easily pass as a full-grown man, but he looked about Boon's age. Kayla's spine tingled. Korey fit the description that Fint Mathis had given of the man with the white mule.

Mazie pointed to Korey and said, "This be Korey. My girl is Pearl."

"Glad to meet you," said Kayla and Timothy just as their mama had taught them.

"What d' they want, Ma?" asked Korey.

"Didn't say," said Mazie, sticking her pipe back in the corner of her mouth.

"They talk funny," said Korey.

Pearl limped to Kayla, reached up with her good arm, and tugged at Kayla's mass of black hair. "Hair, hair," she said in a slow, croaky voice.

Startled, Kayla stepped back, but Pearl hung on. Kayla didn't know what to say or how to act.

"Let that girl be, Pearl!" snapped Mazie.

Pearl limped away and crouched down in the dirt beside the house. The dog sank down beside her, his great head on her bare foot.

"We came on the Orphan Train," said Timothy because he didn't know what else to say. He couldn't just blurt out, "You got our white mule?"

"We came from Ireland," said Kayla. "County Offaly." She was at a loss for words too.

"We're new to Nebraska," said Timothy. What had happened to his great gift of gab?

"We never saw a cowboy 'til we got here," said Kayla.

"You sure do talk funny," said Korey with a bark of a laugh.

Kayla thought *he* talked funny, but she didn't say so. "Are you a cowboy, Korey?"

He puffed up with pride and looped his finger around his overall straps. "Sure am. Ain't I, Ma?"

Mazie pulled out her pipe and waved it around. "Show these kids our place. See that the horses get watered afore they head back." She turned on her heels and walked back inside.

Pearl stood up and walked toward Kayla.

"You get back, Pearl!" snapped Korey. "You don't bother

our company." He turned to Kayla and Timothy. "She's slow some in the head."

Kayla felt bad for Pearl, so she smiled at her before she followed Timothy and Korey across the rutted yard toward the sod barn. Would they see Sterling inside the barn? Her stomach cramped, and she walked faster to keep up with Korey.

He showed them the cattle and bragged about helping brand them last spring. Finally he took them inside the small sod barn. It smelled of manure. "I got me a good luck piece in here," he said, nodding so hard his floppy hat brim slapped his head.

Timothy stopped short, and Kayla bumped into him. They both stared at the white mule in the first stall. Was it Sterling?

"'Tis a fine looking mule you have there," said Timothy when he finally found his voice.

"I call him Lucky," said Korey with great pride.

Kayla stepped closer. Did all white mules look alike? She'd looked at Sterling many times, but she couldn't tell if this mule was Sterling. She noticed the halter was different, but it was easy enough to change halters. Then she saw the tiny nip in the right ear. It *was* Sterling! She forced back the wild thump of her heart and willed Timothy to see the nip.

"You had him long?" asked Timothy as he looked the mule over carefully.

"Long enough," said Korey sharply. He reached out and gently stroked the mule. "My lucky piece." He looked over his thick shoulder at Kayla and Timothy. "Did you know white mules are lucky?"

"How come?" asked Timothy.

"I never knew that," said Kayla.

"You own a white mule and your whole place does good . . . your cattle and your family and everything. I figure my having a white mule will even help Pearl."

Kayla's heart sank. How could Korey put trust in a white mule instead of in God?

"Are there many white mules around?" asked Timothy as he patted the mule. Now that Timothy had horses to work with, he could have a little tolerance for mules. "I might be interested in getting one."

Kayla watched a gray cat sit in the sunlight just outside the barn door and lick its fur. She didn't know if she wanted to hear Korey's answer.

Korey pulled off his floppy hat and scratched his shaggy brown hair. "White mules are scarce as hen's teeth in these parts. I been looking for one a long time."

Timothy's stomach knotted. "I heard there was one over at Bitter Creek Ranch."

Kayla darted a look at Timothy. How daring he was!

Korey clamped his hat back on. "I don't know nothing about that. Don't know nothing about Bitter Creek Ranch."

Kayla wanted to get away from the sod barn and away from Korey Rhoba. If he learned they were from Bitter Creek Ranch he might turn mean. She gave Timothy a warning look, and he nodded slightly to show he understood.

"We have to be going," said Timothy.

"Wait!" Korey caught Timothy's arm, and Kayla's stomach knotted. Korey pulled a gold watch from his front pocket and lifted the cover. Music floated out from it, and Korey looked proudly at Kayla and Timothy to see if they'd heard. They smiled and nodded, and he looked back at the watch. He studied the face a long time, then said, "If you got time

I'll show you my kittens. I might give you one if you ask real nice."

"That's kind of you," said Timothy.

"I like kittens," said Kayla. She wanted to leave, but she walked with the boys to the far corner of the barn to a nest of gray kittens.

Korey picked one up gently and handed it to her.

She cuddled it close and smelled its dusty hair. She rubbed her cheek against its silky body. Suddenly she wished they were there just to enjoy the visit and pet the kittens. She stroked the kitten while Timothy and Korey talked about horses and mules and which was better. Finally Kayla put the kitten back and headed for the door. She couldn't stay another minute.

"Where are you going?" asked Korey sharply.

"Outdoors," she said. "We should be going, shouldn't we, Timothy?"

"That we should," he said. He ran after Kayla. "You got a nice place here, Korey."

"I'll come see you next," he said "Where do you live?"

Kayla caught her breath, and Timothy stumbled and almost fell.

Finally Timothy said, "We can't tell. The folks we live with said not to tell."

"We don't want to get in trouble and get whipped," said Kayla, feeling guilty about not being more truthful.

"Pa whips me sometimes," said Korey, rubbing his backside. "But when he gets back and sees that white mule he won't whip me no more."

"That's good," said Timothy.

"You water your horses before you leave," said Korey. "Ma said you got to."

Her hands trembling, Kayla untied the mares and led them to the tank. They drank forever, it seemed. Finally she swung into the saddle and rode away with a wave of her hand.

A few minutes later she and Timothy rode side by side across the wide valley and up the long hill, then finally out of sight. Timothy pulled up on the reins and wiped his forehead. Kayla breathed a long sigh of relief.

"That's Sterling all right," Timothy said. "I couldn't tell at first, but then I saw that nip out of his right ear."

"Me too," said Kayla. "But I didn't know if you noticed. Let's get back fast and tell Abel."

"And what will he do, him with the crippled leg?"

Kayla shrugged. She hadn't thought that far ahead.

"I say we sneak back and take Sterling home with us."

Kayla sucked in her breath. She would like to do that, since it was her fault the mule was stolen. "But how?"

"That I haven't figured out. But I will." Timothy pulled off his cap and scratched his head. Wind blew a tumbleweed across in front of the mares, and they jerked and nickered.

Another horse nickered, and they froze. Was it Korey's pa? And had he heard them talking?

Timothy nudged his mare forward and Kayla followed, her skin damp with sweat. They rounded a grassy knoll and there stood Boon Russell leading a black gelding. Kayla's pulse leaped, and her nerve ends tingled. She wanted to slide off her mare into Boon's arms, but she sat still and stared at him, her feelings showing in her eyes.

"Boon Russell," she whispered, her mouth suddenly bone-dry.

He smiled up at her. "Kayla! I was afraid I'd never see you again."

"Nor me you," said Kayla softly.

Timothy rolled his eyes as he watched the two. Finally he said, "What brings you out here, Boon?"

He dragged his eyes off Kayla and turned to Timothy. "I know who knocked me out and robbed me."

"Who?" Kayla and Timothy asked in one voice.

"Korey Rhoba." Boon nodded, his face hard. "When I got back to town I suddenly remembered what happened after I rented the buggy. Korey Rhoba was walking out on the prairie, and I stopped to give him a ride. We talked as we traveled, and then he struck me down and robbed me. The man at the livery said the horses came back in with the empty buggy." He motioned toward the black gelding. "This time I rented a horse to bring me out here to get my things back, especially my grandpa's watch."

"Korey has a gold watch on him," said Timothy. "It plays a little melody when it's opened."

"That's Grandpa's watch!" Boon brushed moisture from his eyes and cleared his throat. "I want it back."

"We'll get it for you," said Kayla without knowing just how they'd do it.

"What brings you two out here?" asked Boon "I thought Rachel would have you tied to the ranch, working hard."

"Korey Rhoba stole Sterling," said Kayla. "We found him in their barn."

"You don't say!" Boon said.

"I have a plan!" cried Timothy with a broad smile.

"Count me in," said Boon.

Kayla's eyes sparkled as she leaned toward Timothy to hear his great plan.

A White Mule and a Gold Watch

Kayla crept into the sod barn and over to Sterling. She'd been chosen to lead Sterling away because she knew more about mules than Timothy or Boon. She'd left her mare behind a small hill to the south of the barn and then, bending low in the tall grass, had run to the barn. The dog was her only concern, but Timothy had said he'd tend to the dog.

"I came to take you home, Sterling," Kayla whispered as she snapped a lead rope onto the halter. She opened the stall door and tugged on the rope. Sterling wouldn't budge. "Sterling, 'tis not time to be stubborn. You must be coming with me right now." Still Sterling wouldn't move.

Kayla groaned and darted a look toward the door. Fear pricked her skin. She had to get Sterling out while Boon and Timothy were inside the house talking to Korey and Mazie. How could she make the stubborn white mule move?

Just inside the sod house Boon and Timothy were looking down the barrel of a muzzleloader held in Korey's hands. Mazie and Pearl stood on the far side of a cluttered table, with the big dog next to Pearl. A kerosene lamp burned on the table to give light to the inside of the sod house.

"What trouble you in now, Korey?" asked Mazie with a scowl.

"None, Ma," said Korey.

"You might be," said Timothy with a firm shake of his head. "I came back to warn you."

"Why'd you bring him?" asked Korey, waving the tip of the muzzleloader at Boon.

"He said you might know who robbed him," said Timothy in a kind, patient voice. "Do you?"

Korey shook his head hard.

"You better not know, Korey," said Mazie. "If you do, you know your pa will whip the daylights out of you. Now put that gun back where it belongs and take these boys outside. I got to start dinner." She turned to Pearl. "You take Dog and you go out too."

Pearl nodded hard and awkwardly patted Dog's head. "Come, Dog," she said in her croaky, slow voice.

Korey hesitated, then hung the muzzleloader over the bed.

Timothy's mind whirled with ways to keep them inside just a little longer, long enough for Kayla to get Sterling out of sight of the house. Suddenly an idea leapt into his mind. "I heard a story about a white mule once. Mazie, you'll want to hear this. I'll sit right down here and tell it and you can keep on working." Timothy plopped down on a stool at the cluttered table. "This story is about a man who thought he had a lucky white mule."

Korey was just reaching for his hat that hung on a peg beside the door "White mules are lucky, ain't they, Ma?"

"Sure are," said Mazie "Tell yer story. Pearl, get Dog and

sit down. You'll like this. A story, Pearl . . . about a white mule."

Pearl sank to the floor with Dog across her lap.

Boon frowned. "I don't want to listen to a story 'bout a white mule. I want to talk to Korey about the guy that robbed me."

"Sit down and listen," snapped Mazie, waving the knife she had picked up to peel potatoes with.

Boon looked at Timothy, and he nodded slightly. Boon sank to the edge of the bed.

Timothy racked his brain for details of the tale he was going to tell. "Jake wanted a white mule," Timothy said, "because he always heard white mules were lucky."

"They are," said Korey, nodding. He sat on a stool across from Timothy. The room reeked with his unwashed body.

Mazie stood on the other side of the table peeling potatoes in a pan. "Let him tell the story," she said with her pipe hanging from her lips.

Timothy pulled his cap off and held it in his hands. "Jake decided he wanted a white mule so much that he did something really bad . . . He *stole* a white mule." Timothy waited a minute to let that sink in. Korey moved restlessly.

"Stole it," said Pearl as she rubbed Dog's ears.

"Yes, stole it," said Timothy. "He walked right into someone's barn and took that white mule for luck. What he didn't know was that stealing a white mule makes it unlucky. Things go bad then because stealing is wrong."

"You bet yer boots it's wrong!" said Mazie, her eyes flashing.

"Wrong," said Pearl.

Korey just sat there, rocking slightly.

Timothy glanced at Boon, then back at the others. "The first thing that happened to Jake for stealing that mule was that his pa whipped him hard, and Jake was practically a man. He whipped Jake, then he told Jake to return that mule. But Jake just couldn't bring himself to take that mule back because he was sure he'd be put in jail. And Jake hates being locked up anywhere. He likes open spaces and country living and soft little kittens."

"Kittens," said Pearl..

Mazie turned and patted Pearl gently on the head, then went back to peeling potatoes.

"What else happened?" asked Korey.

Timothy was getting so nervous, he thought every word he knew had left his mind. But he kept talking anyway. He had to give Kayla time to get away with Sterling. "Jake decided he'd take that white mule back. So he went to the barn, but the white mule had disappeared . . . vanished into thin air. He didn't know what to think . . . He didn't know what to do. But he learned his lesson: a stolen white mule is never lucky."

"Never lucky," said Pearl.

Dog lifted his head and whined, then ran to the door.

"Let Dog out, Korey," said Mazie. She looked at Timothy. "Is that all the story?"

"Yes." Timothy's heart sank as he watched Korey walk to the door. "We'll all go out with Dog. Come on, Pearl. Come with Dog." Timothy could see the dog was trained to guard Pearl. If she was outdoors too, Dog wouldn't run to the barn to sniff out Kayla. "Come on, Pearl."

In the barn Kayla frantically tugged on Sterling's lead rope. She was wet with nervous perspiration and almost to the end of her patience. Then suddenly she remembered her grandma telling her mules wouldn't take a step if there was danger. But what danger could there be?

She looked down on the floor just inside the doorway. A board with nails sticking up was lying in a spot that made it impossible for Sterling to step over it without hurting himself. Korey had probably put it there because he knew mules well enough to know that if Sterling could get out, he'd run right back to Bitter Creek Ranch. That board with nails kept Sterling in better than any locked door ever could.

Kayla carefully picked up the board and set it aside, then tugged on Sterling's rope. He stepped right out of the stall and followed her to the door. She peeked out, saw that the coast was clear, and led Sterling away from the barn and toward the small hill. Between the barn and the hill was the danger spot — anyone looking from the house would certainly see them.

"Keep walking, Sterling," she said urgently. This was not the time for Sterling to get a stubborn streak.

Just then Timothy stepped out of the house. He saw Sterling and Kayla, so he stumbled, fell into Korey, and sent them both sprawling back inside. "I'm that sorry!" he cried as he lifted Korey to his feet. He motioned to Boon with his eyes, and Boon quickly blocked the door to keep Pearl and Dog inside.

Timothy brushed off Korey, slipping Boon's watch from Korey's pocket as he did. He'd learned that trick from other orphans who made their living that way.

Boon glanced out just as Kayla disappeared behind the hill with Sterling. He stepped outdoors and breathed deeply. Wind ruffled his red hair.

Timothy walked out with Korey close behind him. "Listen to me, Korey," said Timothy in a hushed voice. "If you get to the barn and find that white mule gone, you be glad. Stolen white mules are not lucky."

Korey nodded hard.

"You save your money and *buy* a white mule," said Timothy.

"White mule," said Pearl.

Timothy smiled at her, shook her good hand, and said, "I am most glad to meet you, Pearl. You have a fine dog there."

Pearl's face twisted, and Timothy knew it was a smile.

"We must go now," said Timothy. He slapped Boon on the back. "Sorry, Boon, but Korey here can't help you any more."

"I sure certain can't," said Korey.

"I wish you could," said Boon.

Timothy mounted his mare and waited for Boon. Then they rode together away from the Rhoba place.

When they were out of sight of the ranch, Boon said, "Did you get it?"

Laughing, Timothy pulled the watch from his pocket and held it out to Boon. "Is this yours? 'Twould be terrible if I stole Korey's very own watch."

Boon chuckled and opened the watch. The music drifted out across the prairie. He closed it and held it close to his heart. "It's my watch . . . my grandpa's. Thanks, Timothy."

"Think nothing of it," said Timothy, but he felt ten feet tall.

"I can do without the cash money he took, but I could

never do without the watch," said Boon as he opened it again just to hear the music.

With Sterling safely at the end of the lead rope, Kayla stopped her mare at the place where they'd found Boon, then waited for Timothy and Boon. Her heart raced with excitement. She had Sterling! And soon she'd see Boon again. "If they got away with Timothy's plan . . ." she said to herself. Timothy had a way about him, and she knew he could wriggle out of any situation — or talk his way out. He had the O'Brian gift of gab all right.

A few minutes later the two came into sight. Kayla laughed as she rode to meet them. "Did you get the watch?" she asked.

"That we did," said Timothy.

Smiling, Boon held it up, then slipped it back into his pocket. "Where to now?"

"Bitter Creek Ranch," said Kayla.

Boon shook his head. "Not me . . . I have to get back to town."

Kayla's eyes filled with tears. "Won't you be visiting us before you go back east?"

He shook his head.

Timothy rolled his eyes. He couldn't stomach all the billing and cooing. "I'll take Sterling and ride a bit ahead to give the two of you some time alone."

"Thank you, Timothy," said Kayla, handing the lead rope to him. "Keep Sterling to the left of your mare and he'll walk along just fine."

"What does it matter?" asked Boon.

"Mules are plumb loco," said Timothy, sounding just like Abel.

Kayla grinned. "A mule has a favored hoof. He steps out first with that hoof, and he wants that hoof on the inside. Sterling's favored hoof is his right, so he wants to be on the left of the mare."

Timothy shook his head, but let Sterling walk on the left side of his mare. They walked along without any trouble at all. "Dumb mule," muttered Timothy.

Kayla fell in beside Boon, and they rode side by side, their legs almost touching. "I was afraid I wouldn't get to be saying good-bye to you," she said.

"I was pretty upset when Rachel left me in town." Boon grinned and lifted a brow. "I had all kinds of plans to get back out to see you, but I never could find the courage because I knew I'd have to face Rachel Larsen."

"She's had a hard life, and it has left her bitter," said Kayla.

"I wish I could be as forgiving as you," said Boon.

"I am that way only with God's help."

Boon was quiet a long time. "Will you write to me?" he finally asked.

"Yes . . . And will you be writing to me?"

Boon nodded. "I'll never forget you, Kayla O'Brian! You saved my life."

"I'm that glad I did."

"Someday when I get everything sorted out at home and when I finish my schooling I'll come back and look you up. I promise you that."

Kayla's eyes filled with tears. "I'll be holding you to that promise, Boon Russell."

He reached out for her hand, and without hesitation she put her hand in his. They rode hand in hand until it was time for Boon to turn toward town and for Kayla to turn toward Bitter Creek Ranch. He squeezed her hand, then let it go.

She sat quietly and watched while he rode off across the vast prairie.

"Let's be going, Kayla," said Timothy softly.

She nodded and nudged her mare forward. "I thank God I could see him to say good-bye," she said.

"Our Father works miracles," said Timothy.

Kayla smiled through her tears. Someday Boon Russell would ride back into her life. She knew that with a knowing as strong as Timothy's ever was.

Sterling's Buyer

Kayla and Timothy laughed excitedly as they rode into the yard with Sterling. The whole family ran to meet them, including Pansy Butler and Czar.

"Where'd you find him?" asked Scott, Jane, and Ula.

Rachel took the lead rope from Timothy and patted Sterling. "You brought him back!" She sounded close to tears.

Abel thumped his cane on the ground. "I told you kids not to do that! I said to come tell me. You could've been shot!"

"But they weren't," said Pansy, grinning at Kayla as she dismounted and shook her skirt down. Pansy hiked up her gunbelt. "I want to hear the whole dangerous tale . . . all of it!"

Rachel looked over her shoulder on the way to taking Sterling to the barn. "Wait'll I get back. I want to hear it too."

Abel shook his finger at Timothy. "I told you not to do that, didn't I?"

Timothy grinned and nodded.

"Timothy had a great plan to get Sterling that didn't put us in too much danger," said Kayla, winking at Timothy.

"We scoured the countryside yesterday, but we didn't see a sign of Sterling," said Greene. "Where was he?"

"At the Rhobas'," said Kayla.

"But we checked there!"

"It's easy enough to hide something you don't want found," said Abel. He sighed heavily. "I told you kids not to take action, but you did, and now it's over and done with." Suddenly he laughed. "And you did good. I'm proud of you both."

Timothy and Kayla smiled happily.

Pansy smacked Abel on the back. "I never thought I'd live to see the day you ever praised anybody."

"A man can change," said Abel softly.

Kayla caught the look of surprise on Rachel's face at Abel's words as she walked toward them. But she quickly masked it.

"You couldn't change if somebody paid you," said Rachel, frowning at Abel.

Abel flushed, but didn't answer back.

Pansy poked Rachel. "You changed . . . from good to bad. It's time you turned back into the sweet girl you used to be."

Kayla had heard all the stories about Rachel from Pansy.

"You once were sweet and kind, too, Mama," snapped Rachel. "What happened to you?"

Kayla had not heard those stories, but under Pansy's gruff exterior she'd seen a gentle woman who loved books and music and animals.

"Enough of this," said Abel. "Let's sit on the porch and

listen to the story. Timothy and Kayla, let's hear those golden Irish tongues of yours."

They all sat together on the long front porch, and Timothy and Kayla told their tale while the warm Nebraska wind blew tumbleweeds across the prairie and whirled the blades of the windmill.

When the story was told Ula said sadly, "I feel sorry for them that they don't have a white mule."

"Me too," said Jane. "But Korey shouldn't have stolen Sterling."

"Stealing is wrong," said Abel. "No matter how bad you want something, you can't steal it."

"I don't think Korey will ever try to steal Sterling again," said Timothy.

"He won't have a chance," said Rachel. "The buyer comes tomorrow. He's a man who knows his mules, and he'll appreciate Sterling and how well he's trained."

The next morning Kayla stood at Sterling's stall. "I'll be missing you, Sterling. Could it be me saying that?" Kayla laughed and patted Sterling's neck. "You're a fine animal even if you are but a mule." She looked over at the three horses in their stalls and smiled. "You can't compare with those beauties, but you're not to be compared now, are you? You're a mule and they are not."

Just then Rachel stormed into the barn. "Abel . . ."

"He's not in here," said Kayla.

"Where is he? I can't find him anywhere."

"I haven't seen him since breakfast."

Rachel scowled and started back toward the door. Suddenly she stopped and turned. "I'm glad you got to say good-bye to Boon," she said in a low voice, her cheeks flushed red.

Kayla smiled. "I am that glad too. He said he'd write to me . . . And I'll be writing to him."

Rachel turned and walked out without another word.

Kayla leaned against Sterling's stall. "Her heart is softening, Sterling. Now if 'twould soften toward Abel we'd have a happy family here at Bitter Creek Ranch."

Later Kayla walked toward the house, then spotted Abel planting two new bushes in place of the ones the horses had torn up. Rachel was watching him.

"Why are you doing this?" Rachel asked sharply.

Abel grinned up at her as he knelt beside a bush. "You liked the bushes, and I felt bad when they got ruined."

"I don't know what's got into you, Abel Larsen!"

Slowly and awkwardly he stood, braced against his cane. "I am no longer the whipped dog I was. I am the man of the house, and I mean to take the responsibility of this ranch and this family the way I should."

Kayla smiled and walked away quietly so they wouldn't notice her.

"It won't last," said Rachel.

"It will," said Abel softly. "I promise you it will." He took a step toward her, but she jumped back.

"Father God, show her how to open her heart to him," whispered Kayla. "And to You."

Abel leaned both hands on his cane and studied Rachel. "I'm going to take care of the buyer when he comes for Sterling. You don't have to concern yourself with him."

Rachel knotted her fists at her sides. "I will handle that buyer today, Abel, and don't you try to stop me."

Abel shook his head. "I told Pansy you'd be over to spend the day with her. I sent Greene to hitch up the buggy for you."

"You don't even know how to handle a buyer," snapped Rachel.

"I know how," Abel said stiffly. "Go visit your mama and rest again today."

"You expect me to rest two days in a row? How will things get done?"

"They'll get done. We got Kayla and Timothy to help."

Rachel spun on her heels and stormed off to the buggy that Greene was driving up.

Abel turned, saw Kayla, and smiled at her.

"I like the bushes," Kayla said with a grin as she walked to Abel's side. "Rachel does too, but she doesn't know how to say it." Kayla motioned to the bushes. "Shall I water them for you?"

Abel nodded. "Soak 'em good. This sandy soil takes a lot of water." Abel pulled off his hat and rubbed his head. "Pansy said she told you about them forcing Rachel to marry me."

Kayla nodded. "She said your wife had died, leaving you with Greene. He was two years old, and you needed a mama for him and a wife for yourself."

"And they didn't want Rachel to run off with that whisky-drinking, irresponsible cowboy Soren Hart she thought she was so in love with." Abel sighed heavily. "She finally forgave her folks just before her father died, but she never forgave me."

"I'm sorry," said Kayla.

"I know you're praying for us, Kayla. You keep it up."

"That I will!"

Just after dinner Scott ran to the porch to tell Abel the buyer was coming. Kayla heard from inside, where she was helping Ula finish the dinner dishes.

Abel stuck his head in the doorway. "Kayla, bring a bill of sale and come with me to the barn."

Kayla dried her hands and grabbed a bill of sale, a pen, and the bottle of ink, then walked to the barn with Abel.

A few minutes later a short wiry man strode into the barn, a toothpick between his lips. He tongued the toothpick to the side of his mouth and said with his hand out to Abel, "Ben Dane here. I've come for the white mule."

"Glad to meet you, Dane. I'm Abel Larsen, and this is my daughter Kayla O'Brian."

Kayla stiffened to be called Abel's daughter. She was Patrick O'Brian's daughter! She managed to smile at Ben Dane as he doffed his hat.

Dane walked to the stall and patted Sterling on the neck. "I'm glad to finally get this mule. I told your missus I'd send a money draft when I get back to my bank."

Abel shook his head. "Sorry. No money, no mule."

Dane frowned as he reached in his pocket for the money. "If that's the way you're gonna be . . ." He noticed Kayla writing out a bill of sale, and he waved it away. "No need for that."

"It's proof you didn't steal it from us," said Abel. "And our copy is proof you bought it from us."

"Just let me have my mule." Dane opened the stall door and grabbed Sterling by the halter. "Come on, mule." He tugged, but Sterling didn't budge.

Kayla frowned thoughtfully. What was the man trying to do? Didn't he know anything about mules? A mule liked to have a chance to step out of the stall at his own pace with his favored hoof.

"Let me give you a hand," said Abel. He snapped a lead onto the halter and led Sterling from the stall.

Kayla followed them outside to Dane's buggy. She held the bill of sale in her hand. She watched Dane take Sterling and tie him to the right of the buggy. Suddenly Kayla stepped to Abel's side and whispered, "Take Sterling back. This man is not the right buyer."

Abel frowned at Kayla, sighed, limped over to Sterling, and untied the rope. "Dane, this mule is not for you. Here's your money back. Take it and be on your way."

Dane shook his head. "I paid good money for that mule, and I mean to take him."

Abel stuffed the money into Dane's hand. "Ride out of here and don't come back."

Dane swore under his breath, climbed in his buggy, and drove away.

Kayla sighed in relief, then laughed.

Abel turned on her. "Just tell me what's going on here."

Kayla told him, "I don't know who that man was, but Rachel said the buyer knew mules. That man knew less about mules than I do. I wonder who he is or who sent him." She took Sterling's lead rope and led him back to his stall.

About an hour later Kayla and Abel watched a man drive into the yard in a two-seater buggy with a black leather top. Rachel sat beside him. They both jumped from the wagon as Kayla and Abel walked to meet them. The man was medium build with a thick black mustache that covered his top lip.

Rachel's cheeks were flushed, and her eyes sparkled with mischief. "This is Mark August. He came for Sterling."

Abel stiffened, darted a look at Kayla, then said innocently, "He's in the barn."

Rachel gasped, and her face turned as white as the

clouds in the sky. With great effort she pulled herself together.

"Shall I get Sterling for you?" asked Kayla. "I can write out the bill of sale too."

"That would be fine," said the man.

A few minutes later Kayla led Sterling to August. He handed the money to Abel and took the bill of sale from Kayla with a smile and a hearty thank you. He led Sterling to the buggy, walked around to the left side, and tied Sterling in place. Rachel had tried to embarrass Abel, but she'd failed.

Without a word they all watched the buggy roll away with Sterling walking along beside it.

When August was out of earshot Rachel turned on Abel with a scowl. "You think you're smart, don't you?"

He shook his head. "Not me . . . Kayla."

Rachel turned on Kayla. "Can't you leave me alone?"

"I want you to be happy," said Kayla just above a whisper.

"So do I," said Abel. "I know how good you are in dealing with buyers and working with mules. I am good with horses and even with business deals. After that trick you pulled, I realized it makes you happy to take care of buyers and train mules. Then you should do it. If we work together instead of being at each other's throats, maybe we can both be happy."

Rachel pulled her hat low and strode to the corral, where Jane was working with the mules.

Abel sighed heavily.

"Don't give up," said Kayla.

"An O'Brian doesn't give up," said Abel with a short laugh. "It's too bad I'm not an O'Brian." He limped toward the house, leaning heavily on his cane. He glanced back and said, "Walk over to Pansy's and drive the buggy back."

Kayla nodded. She walked out into the waving grass with her head high and her back straight. She wouldn't give up on Rachel no matter how Rachel acted. An O'Brian never gives up.

Thanksgiving

Her eyes blurred with tears, Kayla leaned on the corral fence and watched Timothy ride Offaly around. He looked small for the tall chestnut mare, but he kept a firm rein just as Papa had taught him. They'd named her Offaly after the county where they'd come from. It felt good just to say her name. Kayla bit her bottom lip. Cold November wind whipped across the bleak prairie.

The buyers had come the end of last month for the mules that Rachel and Jane had trained in the corral, leaving the area free for Timothy and Kayla to use for the horses.

Timothy rode to the fence and slipped to the ground. He let the reins dangle. Abel had told him the mare was trained to stand in place as long as the reins touched the ground. Timothy sighed heavily, stood on the bottom rail, and leaned against the top. "Not even working with Offaly takes my mind off Mama today."

Kayla quickly brushed her tears away "We can't be crying over Mama's birthday. She wouldn't want that." Kayla's chin quivered. "Oh but I miss her, Timothy . . . And Papa too."

"Papa would have fun with Offaly . . . and with Big Red and Roxie too."

"Sometimes I ache to feel Mama's arms about me," whispered Kayla. "I want to smell her skin and touch her silky hair."

Timothy rubbed the back of his hand across his red nose. "Rachel is not like Mama at all."

"Nor Abel like Papa." Kayla hunched her shoulders against the cold wind. "He called me his daughter, Timothy. I am not his daughter!"

Timothy was quiet a long time. "They signed for us."

"I am an O'Brian, not a Larsen."

"As I am!" Timothy gripped Kayla's hand. "We will always be O'Brians! Nobody can make us be called Larsen."

Kayla squeezed Timothy's hand back. "Never," she vowed.

Just then Greene walked up to them. He looked cold. "Ma said it's time for dinner." He reached through the wooden fence and patted Offaly's neck, thick with winter hair. "Timothy, do you think you could teach me about horses?"

Timothy nodded.

"You'll be good with them," said Kayla. "You have the strength yet the gentleness that it takes."

Greene smiled at her, and for a quick flash she saw love for her in his eyes. It curled warmly around her heart. Today she needed all the love she could get.

Timothy opened the gate and rode Offaly to the barn.

Greene closed the gate and walked to the house beside Kayla. "Why are you so sad today?" he asked.

With a catch in her voice she told him it was Mama's birthday. "We had planned to celebrate her day at Briarwood Farms in Maryland. But she's in Heaven and we're in Nebraska."

"I wish I could make you feel better," he said softly.

"Thank you."

"I'm glad you're here and not in Maryland." He opened the door for her, and she stepped into the warm kitchen with smells of turkey and dressing and pumpkin pie filling the air. Her stomach cramped with hunger, and that surprised her. She thought she was too sad to eat.

Later at the table Abel thanked the Lord for the food, surprising even Kayla. When he lifted his head he smiled at Kayla and Timothy. "We're especially thankful for our two children from Ireland."

"Thank you," Kayla managed to say.

"That we are," said Pansy in the chair Boon would've sat in if he were there. Pansy had come over early to help prepare the feast and to share the day. She had pulled Kayla aside and told her she was thankful to learn her grandchildren were not half-witted as she'd thought. "I'm growing to care for them," she'd whispered in surprise with a low chuckle.

Now Kayla smiled across the table at Pansy as she held the bowl for Scott to spoon out some potatoes.

"What is this whole Thanksgiving Day all about?" asked Timothy.

Scott laughed. "Don't you have Thanksgiving Day in Ireland?"

"No," said Timothy.

"You tell them, Ma," said Jane in a shy, hesitant voice. "I remember when you told me. You tell it good."

Rachel shrugged, and while they ate she told about the Pilgrims and the Indians.

Kayla had never heard Rachel talk so much. Her heart was indeed growing softer. But she'd never be as kind and as good as Mama had been. Suddenly Kayla realized that she couldn't compare the two, just as she couldn't compare mules with horses. Both were different; both had good points. Mama was Mama, and Rachel was Rachel.

Suddenly feeling better, Kayla helped herself to more turkey.

After the dishes were done, Kayla stood at the window and looked out at the gray sky. As she watched, giant snowflakes drifted to the ground and melted immediately. "It's snowing!" she called.

"Oh my," said Pansy. "I have to get home before it gets too bad out."

"Greene, hitch up Grandma's buggy," said Abel. "Be quick about it before that snow gets serious."

Greene grabbed his coat and hat and ran out the door while the snow whirled around him. Czar ran at his heels. Snow was sticking to the ground now, leaving white patches here and there.

Pansy slipped on her long, heavy coat and wrapped her scarf around her neck, then reached for her hat. "If this keeps up, don't anybody try to come help with chores." She looked right at Kayla. "I can manage on my own."

"Ma, maybe you should stay," said Rachel, frowning out at the snow.

"It's only a mile to my place."

"But the storm could turn into a blizzard before you get home. It's happened before." Rachel turned to Abel. "See if you can talk her into staying."

"You know you're welcome, Pansy," said Abel.

She patted his arm. "That's good to know, but I got to get home."

Timothy touched Kayla's hand. "Go with her, Kayla."

Kayla looked into Timothy's face, and she knew this

was one of his times of knowing something before it happened. "I will go with you now," said Kayla.

"I'd be glad for the company, but there's no need for you to go out in that weather."

"Kayla, take along your night things and stay the night with her," said Rachel. "I'd feel better then."

Kayla dashed upstairs and stuffed her overnight things into her bag, along with Mama's diary and Bible. At Pansy's she'd have a chance to read them in private — something she hadn't done since sharing a bedroom with Jane and Ula.

Just a few minutes later she sat in the buggy beside Pansy, with cold snow whirling around her and nipping her nose and turning her cheeks red. She watched the team of mules flick their ears against the snow. Czar sat on the buggy floor at Pansy's feet, helping keep her legs and feet warm.

"I'll make you popcorn when we get home," said Pansy in a loud voice Kayla could hear over the creak of the buggy.

"Thanks," said Kayla. Pansy had made popcorn for her one day last week when Kayla had helped with her chores. She had liked the taste of it, especially with a crisp apple to go with it.

The sky was full of snow, and the ground was covered with it, making everything in sight white.

"How can you see?" asked Kayla.

"I can't," said Pansy. "But the mules know the way home. They won't make a wrong step."

Kayla shivered with cold. Her feet felt like blocks of ice. She strained her eyes to see Pansy's place and finally did when they were almost on top of it. The mules stopped just outside the barn. Kayla jumped down, and her feet tingled. She felt all thumbs as she unharnessed the mules.

"I'll take care of the chickens," called Pansy as she

walked toward the chicken house with her head down and her hand on Czar's shoulder.

Kayla shivered as she led the mules inside to their stalls. She fed and watered them, her breath hanging in the air in front of her.

When she stepped outside the barn again, the whole world was white. She couldn't see the buggy that she knew was sitting just a short distance away. She swallowed hard. Had Pansy finished with the chickens and gone to the house, or was she still outside in the snow?

Kayla cupped her gloved hands around her mouth and shouted, "Pansy . . . Pansy . . . are you out here?" There was no answer. "Czar . . . Czar, do you hear me?" Kayla listened hard, but the silence was so great that she felt as if she were inside a soundproof white box.

Shivers ran down Kayla's spine. Panic rose inside her as she looked all around. "Don't be getting silly now, Kayla O'Brian," she muttered. "Thank You, Heavenly Father, for Your help and protection. Give me a clear head now when I need it the most."

She stood with her back to the barn door and looked to where she knew the chicken house was. Should she walk to the chicken house to check on Pansy, or should she go right to the house? "The house," she mumbled with a firm nod. She turned in the direction of the house, but she couldn't see it, not even a dark outline of it. She ducked into the wind and ran toward the house. Snow clung to her eyelashes and wet her face. *Shouldn't I have reached the house already*? she wondered. She glanced back. Her footprints were already covered with new snow. Had she passed the house . . . Was she heading out into the prairie where she would wander without finding shelter until it was too late?

Just then she heard a sound. She walked toward it and could make out the ringing of a bell. Pansy had shown her the silver hand bell Tooky had bought her a year before he died. The sound was clear and melodious and beautiful. Kayla's heart leaped within her, and she laughed aloud. Pansy was ringing the bell to guide her!

Kayla followed the bell and finally bumped against the porch. She stumbled up it and found the door. It was open, and Pansy was standing there ringing the bell. Czar stood beside her like a big guard dog. They were both covered with snow.

"Kayla," whispered Pansy, sagging against the doorpost. "The blizzard hit so hard and fast, I didn't know if you'd make it. I prayed and I rang."

"'Tis that glad I am you did!" Kayla stepped inside and it was just as cold there as it had been outdoors, but at least here she could see more than giant white flakes of snow.

Pansy shut the door and set the bell on the kitchen table. She turned to Kayla, shrugged, then wrapped her arms around Kayla's waist.

Kayla looked down at Pansy in surprise, then bent down and hugged her back. Pansy didn't smell like Mama or feel like Mama, but the hug was full of love just like Mama's.

Pansy stepped back and brushed moisture from her eyes. "I best get that stove going or we'll be two chunks of ice before we know it." She lit a lamp, and it cast a soft glow over the room.

With her coat and hat still on, Kayla started a fire in the potbelly stove in the front room while Pansy built the fire in the kitchen range. Kayla carried wood from the shed hooked to the back of the house into the kitchen and front room, dropping the chunks in the woodboxes. Fire crackled in the stoves and finally took the chill from the rooms.

Pansy sank down onto a kitchen chair, sighed heavily, and waved Kayla onto the chair across from her. Czar sank to Pansy's feet, his head on his front legs. "I'm not as young as I used to be, Kayla. I'm glad you were here to help me."

"Timothy knew you'd be needing me," said Kayla.

Pansy shook her head. Her thin gray hair stuck out all over from pulling her hat off. "You and Timothy were sent here," said Pansy. "A long time ago I believed in God. Down through the years things went bad and times were hard, and I worked from dawn 'til dark without time to spend thinking of God or praying. I got bitter and hard and so lonely that I couldn't tolerate life." Pansy rubbed her wrinkled cheek. "Being lonely seems to suck the life right out of you."

Kayla knew all about being lonely.

Pansy unbuttoned her coat but left it on. "Kayla, you brought a breath of fresh air back into my life." The words seemed to come hard for Pansy, but she continued anyway. "You reminded me that there is a God who cares for me. Thank you, Kayla O'Brian."

"You're welcome," whispered Kayla, gratefully receiving the love she felt flowing from Pansy Butler. It helped take the edge off her loneliness for Mama and Papa.

Pansy fingered the silver bell, then looked at Kayla again. "Don't give up on Rachel. She once was full of love . . . And she can be again. If you can break through my hard shell, you can crack hers wide open."

Kayla folded her hands on the table and leaned toward Pansy. "I will keep praying. That I will!"

A Trip to Spade

Kayla sat in the back of the buggy with Timothy and the Larsen children. All the snow was gone. The sky was as bright a blue as Timothy's eyes, and the wind was warm enough to melt the ice in anyone's blood.

This morning Rachel had announced that since it was a nice day the whole family could go to town. She had a meeting with some buyers, and she needed to stock up on supplies in case they couldn't get to Spade until spring. They had stopped by to take Pansy, but she'd wanted to stay home. She gave Rachel her list of needs and waved them on their way.

"We're almost there," said Greene. He'd made sure he got to sit beside Kayla, and that pleased her.

"Maybe I'll have a letter from Boon waiting for me," said Kayla.

Greene scowled. "You won't."

"Why do you say that?"

"He's not a man of his word."

Sparks flew from Kayla's eyes. "Don't be saying bad things about him, Greene Larsen."

Greene flushed and ducked his head.

Kayla felt bad for snapping at him, but she wouldn't tell him so. He should not say bad things about Boon Russell!

Just outside of town they stopped to let a herd of cattle cross the road. The cattle bellowed and bellowed, and one cow stopped right in front of the team of mules.

Timothy crawled back to Kayla and said, "Look over there! See the people in that yard?"

Kayla nodded, then gasped. "'Tis Clare from the Orphan Train."

"That's the family that took her. She must live there." Timothy turned to Greene. "Do you know who lives there?"

"The Petre family," said Greene.

"See that redheaded girl?" said Kayla. "She came on the Orphan Train with us." Kayla waved hard, but Clare didn't seem to see her. She didn't wave, nor did any of the others. "Maybe they are watching the cattle and didn't notice us here," Kayla muttered. Clare had not been a friend, but it was still exciting to see her because she had been with them all the way from New York City. When they'd first started the journey, Clare had warned Kayla to stay away from her boyfriend Bobby. Kayla had happily done so, but Clare was still jealous because Bobby kept looking at Kayla.

"The Petre family keeps the town cows," said Greene.

"What does that mean?" asked Timothy.

"The folks in town that have cows keep them in the pasture at the Petres'. It's on the outskirts of town and quick to get to. Somebody from each family comes to milk his own cow every morning and every night. They pay the Petres for keeping them."

Kayla thought that was a smart idea. She hadn't

thought before about how the town people got their milk. In New York City a man driving a milk wagon had delivered it.

Finally the road was clear, and Abel clucked to the mules and slapped the reins on their backs. He drove down the dusty main street and stopped outside the general store. He turned around and looked at the kids. "Be back here in an hour. Greene, you keep watch on Scott. Jane, you take Ula with you."

Rachel climbed down from the buggy, adjusted her bonnet, brushed her skirt off, and walked down the wooden sidewalk to the big white building that said BOARDING HOUSE. Her meeting with the buyers would be in the dining room of that building.

After the others were out, Kayla stared to climb from the wagon, but Greene reached up and helped her down. She smiled at him, no longer angry. He smiled back, and the smile touched her heart more than she wanted to admit.

She hurried into the general store, where Abel had said they'd get their mail. She stopped at the counter and asked the clerk, "Is there mail for anyone at Bitter Creek Ranch? . . . For me? I'm Kayla O'Brian."

The clerk looked behind him at the cubbyholes and finally pulled out a thin letter addressed to Abel Larsen. "I got one here for Pansy Butler too if you want to take that."

"Thank you," said Kayla in a weak voice. She carried the letters to Abel, who was already looking at warm winter shirts.

"Any word from Boon?" Abel asked.

Kayla shook her head. She couldn't trust herself to speak; she might start to cry.

She walked listlessly around the crowded store. Just then she glanced out the window. The boy walking past looked just like Boon Russell. She looked closer. It was Boon! Her heart almost jumped from her chest. She ran outdoors and called, "Boon!"

He turned and saw her, hesitated a second, then ran back to her. He caught her hands and squeezed them tightly. "Kayla . . . What're you doing in town?"

She tugged her hands free, suddenly self-conscious about her bold display of emotion in a public place. "I should be asking you that. You said you were going back to Vermont."

He blushed. "And I was . . . I still am. But I had to make some money to buy a train ticket."

"But why didn't you come see me?"

"I thought about it, but just couldn't do it."

"Oh," she said weakly. "Could we be having some time together now while I'm here?"

He pulled out his grandpa's watch and clicked it open. Music drifted out over the quiet street. He looked at the time and closed it. "I can give you five minutes."

Her heart sank. Five minutes! It was not nearly enough time to say all that was in her heart. Yet, five minutes was better than no time at all. "Where are you working?" she asked as they slowly walked down the sidewalk.

"At the livery . . . cleaning stalls."

"And how long before you have enough for your train fare?"

"Forever, it seems."

"Maybe I could help you."

Boon looked at her in surprise. "How?"

"Abel gave me spending money . . . I could let you borrow it. You could pay it back when you first write to me."

She pulled a hanky from her pocket, untied it, and

lifted out a silver dollar. She kept the half-dollar for herself. "Here, Boon . . . 'tis yours."

He took it, frowned, then pushed it back into her hands. "No, Kayla, I can't take it . . . I don't know when I'd ever be able to return it."

Her heart almost burst with love for him and his fine manly conduct. She tied the money back into her hanky again.

"I must go now, Kayla."

"Now?"

"I must."

"Will you come see me?"

"If I can . . . It's a long way to the ranch."

"Less than an hour."

"And winter's on us."

"'Tis a fine day today."

He looked across the street, suddenly acting very nervous. "I must go, Kayla. If I can, I'll visit."

She caught his hand and hugged it to her. "Good-bye, Boon. God go with you."

He smiled and ran across the street and down to the livery barn.

In a daze she walked back to the general store. She forced herself to buy a dress since hers were worn out. Finally she found a rich green one made of fine wool. She tried it on in the back room. It felt good against her skin. It nipped in at the waist and fit in all the right places instead of hanging on her like Mama's dresses did. She smiled in the looking glass, then decided to leave the dress on just in case she saw Boon again before they left Spade.

When she walked outside the store, Jane and Ula

stopped her. They'd already found the clothes and boots they needed.

"Want to walk with us?" asked Jane.

"No thanks," Kayla said, looking down toward the livery. She wanted to be alone in case Boon had time for her.

A few minutes later Greene, Timothy, and Scott asked if she wanted to walk around with them. Timothy wore a fine new cowboy hat and boots just like Greene's. Kayla could tell he was proud of them.

"There's a fine horse near the church I want to show you," said Timothy.

She shook her head and walked on, drawing closer to the livery. She wanted just one more glimpse of Boon. If he wasn't busy, maybe he'd have a few more minutes to spare to talk.

Just then she saw Clare step out of the livery. Kayla stopped short. Clare was laughing and brushing her hair back into place with her hands. As Kayla watched, Boon stepped out, caught Clare to him, and kissed her right on the lips!

Kayla gasped. Her legs started giving way, and she leaned heavily on the hitching rail that lined the street. Boon had kissed Clare!

What if they looked up and saw her? With a strangled sob Kayla turned and walked back toward the general store.

Heartache

Kayla leaned against Roxie's stall and burst into tears. For the past three days each time she thought of Boon she'd cried. She made sure no one was around when she broke down because she didn't want to answer any questions. She didn't want the others to know about Boon and Clare — especially Greene. He had been right about Boon. Timothy had tried to speak to her several times, but she'd brushed him aside.

"Oh, Boon," whispered Kayla.

Just then Rachel walked into the barn, her long coat flapping about her legs. It was cold out again, and snow seemed close at hand.

Kayla quickly brushed away her tears and turned her back to Rachel.

"What's the matter?" asked Rachel. "Is something wrong with one of your horses?" Rachel always referred to the three horses as Kayla's, Timothy's, and Abel's. She hadn't so much as looked at them.

Kayla shook her head. She tried to rub her tears away, though she knew that would make her eyes red and puffy.

Rachel walked up to Kayla. "Look at me, Kayla."

Slowly Kayla turned.

Rachel's eyes widened in surprise. "You're crying. I thought you were too strong to cry."

Kayla pulled a hanky from her pocket and wiped her nose.

"What's wrong?" asked Rachel. "Tell me."

Kayla leaned heavily against the stall.

"Tell me, Kayla!"

Kayla's lips quivered. "I saw Boon Russell in town."

Rachel frowned. "I thought he went back east."

"He said he was going to."

"Oh?" Rachel sounded like she understood everything. "Do you feel bad that he didn't come see you?"

"Yes."

"And?"

Kayla didn't want to tell Rachel of all people, but she couldn't hold the words back. They rushed out against her will. "I saw him kissing Clare, the girl from the Orphan Train!"

Rachel rolled her eyes. "Is that all?"

Anger shot through Kayla. "Is that all? 'Tis more than I can bear!"

"Oh, pshaw!"

"How can you be so coldhearted? You lost your true love — that cowboy Soren Hart."

Rachel's face blanched. "Don't mention his name."

"Why? Can that hurt you?"

"Stop it!"

Kayla knew she was wrong to hurt Rachel so, but she was past caring. "He was no good and your papa knew it. That's why he forced you to marry Abel. You have a man who loves you, but you spurn it for the memory of a bad cowboy."

Rachel grew very still. "What makes you think Abel loves me?"

"I've seen it on his face . . . heard it in his voice."

"You're wrong."

Kayla lifted her chin. "I am right! You could see and hear for yourself if you'd let go of your anger and bitterness."

Rachel sank back against the stall. "I don't know what to say."

"Unlock the words in your heart and you'll know." Kayla wheeled around and headed for the door. She looked back over her shoulder. Wind whistled through the rafters of the barn. A cat rubbed against Rachel's ankles, but she ignored it. "Rachel, it's time to find what to say to Abel so you don't have to go all your life being mean and hateful to your family."

Kayla ran to the house and up the stairs to the girls' room. She knew Jane and Ula were busy, so she'd have a few minutes to herself. She fell across the bed and burst into tears.

After a long time the door opened. She looked up to see Rachel walking in. Kayla quickly brushed away her tears and sat up, bracing herself for Rachel's angry, mean words.

Rachel sat beside her. "Kayla, I'm sorry for hurting you."

Kayla stared in surprise.

"I was wrong." Rachel absently played with a loose button on her dress. "Don't let Boon Russell ruin another minute of your life. It's not worth it. I should know." She took a deep steadying breath. "I locked my heart away until it turned to stone." She looked into Kayla's eyes. "But you and Timothy came here and pecked away at my heart until it cracked open. I was surprised to find a real heart inside that heart of stone." She bit her lip, then continued, "A real heart . . . A heart full of love."

As the words Rachel was saying sank in, Kayla felt fresh tears building up, this time tears of gratitude.

"Don't let Boon hurt you further. Remember, you're more than a conqueror through Christ. I've heard you say that dozens of times." Rachel patted Kayla's hand. "And you're an O'Brian! I've heard you say that hundreds of times!"

"That I am!" Kayla thought about the harsh words she'd spoken to Rachel, and she said, "I'm sorry for being so bad to you . . . I had no right."

"It's over and done . . . and it helped me."

"But I should've put a guard on my tongue." Kayla smiled hesitantly. "Thank you for helping me anyway, Rachel."

"I came to thank *you.*" Rachel jumped up. "Dinner's almost ready. I'll see you at the table." She walked out, her skirts flipping around her boots.

Kayla sniffed hard and brushed off her damp cheeks. "Thank You, Heavenly Father," she whispered. "Forgive me for holding my hurt and anger when I knew to rid myself of it. You're so patient with me, and I'm thanking You for that too."

Several minutes later Kayla walked downstairs for dinner. She'd changed into her new green wool dress and had brushed her hair to hang down her back and over her shoulders. She sat at her place with her head high and her blue eyes sparkling.

Grinning, Timothy winked at her and whispered, "I knew you'd get that happy smile back again."

"It's that sorry I am for pushing you away, Timothy."

Just then Abel bowed his head and thanked the Lord for the food. This time no one was surprised.

When he finished, Rachel stood up. Her cheeks were red, and her face had a determined look. "I have something important to say before we eat."

Kayla locked her hands in her lap while the others stared at Rachel in surprise.

Rachel walked slowly around the table and stopped beside Abel. He looked questioningly at her. Slowly she bent, took his face in her hands, and kissed him. "I love you," she said with a catch in her voice.

Tears pricked Kayla's eyes. Timothy reached over and gripped her hand.

Abel pushed back his chair and stood. "Rachel, you picked a fine time to say that to me." He pulled her close and kissed her soundly.

"Hooray!" shouted Timothy.

Kayla was too choked up to speak. She watched the Larsen kids stare at Rachel and Abel in shock, then look away in embarrassment. She wanted to tell them to enjoy the love they saw, but she knew she could say it another time.

Later as they finished dinner Kayla smiled at everyone gathered around the table. "Timothy and I are proud to be O'Brians, but Larsen is a fine name too."

"That it 'tis," said Abel, copying the O'Brians. Everyone laughed. "I for one am proud to be a Larsen, but prouder still to know I have a fine wife who is also a Larsen." He smiled at Rachel, and she smiled back. "And good kids." He smiled at them, and they smiled back. For once Greene didn't blush.

"This will be a busy winter," said Rachel as she spooned

corn onto her plate. "I promised when I signed for Kayla and Timothy that they could go to school and to church. Since we live too far away to do either during the winter, we'll have church and school right here."

Kayla thought her heart would burst with happiness. "I'll be glad to help teach," she said.

"And I'll teach about horses," said Timothy. "We can't be knowing only mules on this fine ranch."

Kayla laughed along with the others.